tell
it to
Naomi

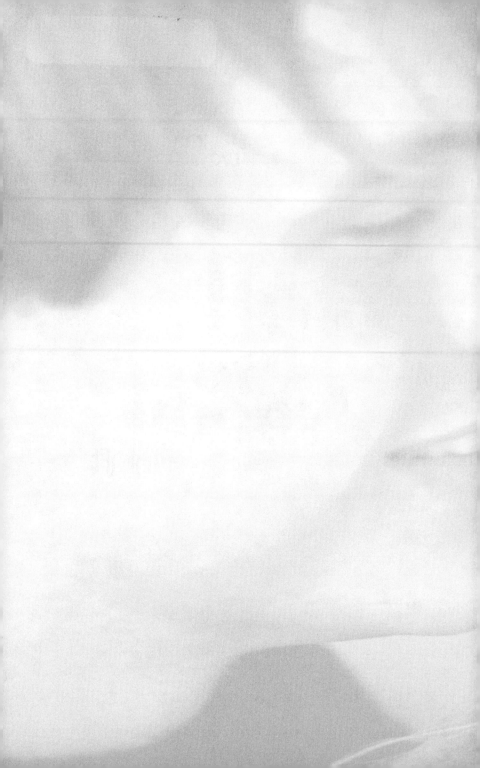

tell it to Naomi

Daniel Ehrenhaft

Delacorte Press

Published by
Delacorte Press
an imprint of
Random House Children's Books
a division of Random House, Inc.
New York

Visit us on the Web! www.randomhouse.com/teens
Educators and librarians, for a variety of teaching tools,
visit us at www.randomhouse.com/teachers

Library of Congress Cataloging-in-Publication Data
Ehrenhaft, Daniel.
Tell it to Naomi / Daniel Ehrenhaft.
    p. cm.
Summary: In a harebrained scheme concocted by his neurotic older sister to forge a romantic relationship with the girl of his dreams, fifteen-year-old Dave Rosen pretends to be a female advice columnist for his school newspaper.
    ISBN 0-385-73129-9 (trade paperback)—ISBN 0-385-90155-0 (GLB) [1. Advice columns—Fiction. 2. Brothers and sisters—Fiction. 3. Interpersonal relations—Fiction. 4. Friendship—Fiction. 5. High schools—Fiction. 6. Schools—Fiction. 7. Jews—United States—Fiction. 8. New York (N.Y.)—Fiction. 9. Humorous stories.] I. Title. PZ7.E3235Te 2004 [Fic]—dc22

                                                                2003014447

The text of this book is set in 11-point Transit 551 Md. Bt.

Book design by Kenny Holcomb

Printed in the United States of America

June 2004

10 9 8 7 6 5 4 3 2 1

BVG

For jessica

Acknowledgments

I would like to thank Wendy Loggia, Jennifer Unter, Ezra Fitz, and, of course, the greatest in-house editor on the planet: my wife, Jessica.

I would also like to thank my parents, my siblings and their families, the Wollmans, and the Charaps for endless inspiration, love, and places to crash.

Finally, I would like to thank the complete discographies of Led Zeppelin, the Butthole Surfers, and Digital Underground.

Prologue ▬▬▬▬▬▬▬▬▬▬▬▬▬▬

Time: 2:23 pm

Subject: fat for halloween

dear naomi,

okay now I'm seriously pissed off and I'm not joking
around anymore. my boyfriend is acting even more
HEINOUS THAN USUAL. my parents are letting me throw
this halloween party tonight, and he says he just
knows that I'm going to buy tons of candy for it, like
this is WRONG. i mean, it's f***ing halloween. (I put
in the asterisks because I know you say not to swear in
the letters.☺) anyway he told me that if I stuff
myself with chocolate bars and gummy worms, which i
have no intention of doing, my butt will get bigger. he
actually SAID this to me. can you believe it? i'm
tempted to hook up an i.v. of chocolate directly to my
butt right now, just to make him mad. it's MY BUTT. i
have the right to make it as fat as I want, right?
meanwhile, he wants to sneak in beer so we can all get
"wasted." HELLO?? beer has like 5 billion times more
calories than candy. what do I do? did YOU ever have to
deal with a loser like this when you were my age? do I
finally dump him? arrrrgh! this may be it. i hate beer.

eagerly awaiting your reply,

s.o.m.b.

1

That was the last e-mail I got before I quit and told everyone the truth.

"S.O.M.B." was one of my regulars. She wrote to me maybe three times a week. The initials stood for "Sick of My Boyfriend." She relied on my help to deal with him. I was her advice columnist, after all. But I was more than that. I was her friend, her confidant—someone she could turn to in secret when she couldn't go to anyone else. I owed her my help.

I owed lots of girls my help.

There was only one problem. (Actually, there were about a zillion problems, but they were all related to one big problem.)

I wasn't Naomi.

Naomi was my glamorous, raven-haired twenty-two-year-old sister.

I was Dave Rosen—her gangly, unglamorous fifteen-year-old brother—and S.O.M.B. didn't know it.

Nobody did.

Chapter One

The whole sordid fiasco began when I saw Celeste Fanucci for the first time—in the hall at Roosevelt High, the second day of school my sophomore year.

I recognized her right away. I'd heard people whispering about her the day before, so I knew what to look for. Not that I had any hope of *talking* to her, of course. No, that would have required major outside help: a sudden celebrity appearance, skeletons rising from their graves, that sort of thing. Only then could I have come up with a good opening line—like, "Hey, it's the guy from that movie!" or, "Watch out: the undead!"

Celeste Fanucci was beautiful. She was mysterious: a new senior, a transfer. She wore a flowery dress and Birkenstocks. Her blond hair tumbled in curly waves down her back.

She had a nose ring. She was cool. She was bohemian. She was a woman.

I was a *boy*.

I was nothing.

You can't exaggerate the chasm that exists between sophomore boys and senior girls. You really can't. It's unbridgeable. Sophomore boys and senior girls aren't even members of the same species. Our species is puny, skinny, and awkward. It's basically designed to be avoided or ignored. Theirs is *ideal*. Theirs appears in commercials. As such, they can do whatever they want. The future stretches at their feet like a red carpet, plush and well vacuumed, leading them straight into a glamorous VIP event—and, farther down the line, into a backstage area patrolled by beefy security guards whose sole job is to keep us sophomore boys away from it.

Okay, I know. Not every senior girl is an unattainable beauty—especially not at Roosevelt High. I mean, if you went to my school, you'd probably say: What about Olga Romanoff, the president of the literary club? *She's* a senior, right? Doesn't she remind you of those Russian dolls, the squat little wooden ones that come packed one inside the other?

And on the flip side, you might say that not all sophomore boys are little wieners, either. There *are* guys like Jed Beck: swarthy, dark— the J. Crew model type. Last year he grew a beard just to show off. He was barely fourteen. The hair came in pretty full, too. Rumor has it that he even bridged the unbridgeable chasm. (With whom, I don't know. Olga Romanoff, I hope.)

But trust me, by the age of twenty-seven Jed Beck will be fat, bald, and miserable—a divorced gas station attendant—whereas I will be the next Jimi Hendrix. Well, except that I won't be black. But I *will* be cool. And I will drive women crazy. I have Faith in this. I really do, as surely as rabbis and priests have Faith in the God they never see in person. I must have Faith. Without it I would lose Hope. And that would just be too depressing to think about.

***

Before I go any further, there's something you should know about me: certain people rag on the way I talk.

According to the Jed Becks of the world, I don't talk the way most "normal" guys do. Whatever. Maybe it's true, but it's not my fault. I've never lived with a guy. I've always lived in a Lower East Side apartment full of insane females—Naomi, my mom, and my mom's twin sister, Ruth. My dad died when I was three. He was a schmuck. He split right after I was born, gallivanting across the country and drinking Jack Daniel's until his liver exploded. In the words of "Papa Was a Rolling Stone" by the Temptations: *When he died, all he left us was alone.*

In case you were wondering how I know the lyrics to a Temptations song that came out almost twenty years before I was born, I have a good excuse: my mom and Aunt Ruth inhabit a bizarre parallel universe where a woman can be both celibate Jewish ogre and funky, aging hippie—and there is no contradiction. This duality somehow makes sense.

As far as I know, no such universe exists outside the confines of 433 East Ninth Street, apartment 4R. I pray it doesn't, anyway. I pray for the rest of humanity's sake.

But back to the second day of school.

Celeste Fanucci must have caught me staring. She flashed me a quick smile and waved.

I bolted.

In my defense, I was already a little late for Algebra II. (Mr. Cooper likes to "make examples of the tardy.") But to tell you the truth, I was heartbroken. She'd just quashed any far-fetched hope I might have had about her, about *us.* Because with that one breezy gesture, she'd said, "You can talk to me—in a little-brotherly way, of course—and I might take you under my wing for five minutes and maybe muss your hair once or twice, like a dog. But don't even *think* about anything else."

I shouldn't have stared at her for so long, I guess. I should have just gone up and said hi.

* * *

One more thing you should know about me, and this is very important: my family has always had a problem with secrets.

By *problem* I mean that our secrets invariably go public—in large part because Naomi always blabs—and when they do, they never fail to disgrace us.

I cite my grandpa Meyer's secret as an example.

Grandpa Meyer was Mom and Aunt Ruth's father. For as long as I knew him, he lived in a retirement home in Brooklyn. He wore a greasy silver toupee. He talked out of the left side of his mouth, like a gangster. He sunned himself whenever possible, too, so his skin had the look and feel of an old baseball mitt.

People say that he was a lot like me.

I don't really see how. I hate the sun. I can go whole summers without swimming or taking off my shirt once, and I'll still be perfectly happy. My skin is superpale. My hair is brown. (Plus it's real.) And I talk fairly normally, if not like other guys. To look at Grandpa Meyer and me—if he were still alive, that is—you probably, *hopefully,* wouldn't even think that we were part of the same family.

The only real similarity I can think of is that he was one of two children, and his older sister was also named Naomi.

In my experience, people tend to see the smaller picture when it comes to relatives. They'll say that one relative is like the other for a few stupid reasons while ignoring all the many reasons they're not alike. People are funny that way.

Anyway, Grandpa Meyer was famous for two things: sneezing and discussing his memoirs. Often they went hand in hand. He would be sitting on the back patio at the retirement home sunning himself and talking out of the side of his mouth. Suddenly he would freeze up. He would stare at a fixed point in space. Then his eyes would narrow . . . and that's when the leathery nose would explode with the force of cannon fire: *Ah-choo! Ah-choo! Ah-choo!*—always three violent bursts in rapid succession, usually followed by several more.

"Bless you!" one of us would shout.

Grandpa Meyer sneered at this.

"Bless you?" he scoffed. "You act as if I did something wrong. Sneezing is a thing of majesty. A sneeze never stands alone. It comes in waves, in chains . . . like the tide, or the Himalayas. I'm going to address this very misconception about sneezing in my memoirs. Then you'll see. You'll all see the truth."

He said this last part with great foreboding.

Needless to say, the four of us were very curious to read these memoirs. After hearing about them for so long, we'd begun to think that maybe Grandpa Meyer was some kind of closet genius or closet madman. (Or closet idiot, I suppose.) But he kept them locked away in a chest in his room. He guarded them jealously until the day he died—of a heart attack while playing blackjack on a seniors-only gambling boat named *Luck Be My Lady.*

I was eight years old; Naomi was fifteen.

At the funeral one of Grandpa Meyer's friends mentioned that he had been holding an ace and a queen when he collapsed. Sadly, he never got to play his hand. "Luck *was* his lady that day," the friend said. "But like all good things, even luck must come to an end." The rest of Grandpa Meyer's cronies nodded in somber agreement. Many of them wore toupees, too.

After Grandpa Meyer was buried, we all scurried back to the retirement home to sit shivah. As harsh as this may sound, though, we weren't really there to mourn. We kept exchanging glances. The air was thick with the unspoken question: *When are we going to get our hands on those memoirs?* Finally Aunt Ruth couldn't take it anymore. She pulled my mother, Naomi, and me aside and whisked us up to his room.

The chest was under his bed. It was padlocked. Aunt Ruth dragged it out and took a hairpin to it.

"Your grandpa wouldn't mind," Mom said.

Neither Naomi nor I disagreed.

When Aunt Ruth finally managed to jimmy the lock and pry open the creaky wooden lid, my heart was pounding—as if we were the original Israelites standing before the Ark of the Covenant.

A great cloud of dust billowed from inside the chest.

Aunt Ruth pulled out a yellowed stack of papers. She straightened quickly and held them up to her glasses. Mom and Naomi huddled on either side of her, blocking my view.

I kept trying to get a look. I couldn't. I was too short.

All at once their jaws dropped.

"My God," Aunt Ruth whispered.

"I don't believe it," Mom said.

Naomi clapped her hand over her mouth. Then she burst out laughing. "Grandpa Meyer!" she shrieked with delight. "You *freak!*"

"What?" I asked desperately. I stood on tiptoe and craned my neck. "What?"

Aunt Ruth didn't answer. She tossed the stack of papers back into the chest and slammed the lid shut. *Smack!* Another cloud of dust arose.

"What's going on?" I demanded. "What's the problem?"

"Nothing," Mom said. She looked pale. "It's just that . . . well, your grandpa Meyer's memoirs aren't appropriate for children."

I shook my head, baffled. "Why not? I thought they were about sneezing."

"Your grandpa used sneezing as a metaphor for . . . something else," she muttered.

Meh-tah-four? I'd heard this word once or twice before, but it was meaningless, a riddle. "I don't get it," I said. "Why can't I see what he wrote? Naomi did."

"Your grandpa's memoirs are somewhat erotic," Aunt Ruth explained.

Mom gave her a disapproving look.

Nobody was making any sense. I wasn't just frustrated anymore; I was starting to get angry. "What does *erotic* mean?"

"It means porn," Naomi said. She was still laughing.

"Naomi!" Mom and Aunt Ruth barked in unison.

"What?" Naomi said defensively. "It *does.*" She pursed her lips. "You know, I don't understand you two. You always insist on using a big word when a four-letter word will do. *Posterior* instead of *butt. Children* instead of *kids. Erotic* instead of *porn.* There's no point in trying to be polite about what Grandpa Meyer was doing. I know you'll probably say that it was 'eccentric.'" She made little quotation marks in the dusty retirement home air to emphasize her disgust.

"But it wasn't. It was sick. *S-I-C-K.* Not to mention funny as hell. And personally, I can't wait to tell everyone."

Mom and Aunt Ruth buried their faces in their hands.

Naomi laughed again.

Even then I knew that my sister was too smart for her own good.

Chapter Two ▬▬▬▬▬▬

"So I hear you want to bang some hot new senior chick."

That was how Naomi greeted me when I got home from school the second day of sophomore year. Luckily, Mom and Aunt Ruth weren't back from work yet. I was still a little out of breath. I'd just climbed four flights of stairs with my book bag. (A sad fact: though our apartment is spacious for a Lower East Side three-bedroom, our building has no elevator.) Naomi was in the kitchen, picking at a jar of olives. She spat the pits into the sink. Her dyed-black hair was a mess. She looked as if she'd rolled right out of bed.

I frowned at her. "How do *you* know?"

She smiled. "Remember my friend Joel Newbury? He just started teaching at Roosevelt. He designed his own literature and creative writing course."

A vague memory drifted through my mind . . . Joel: a pretentious, goateed ex-boyfriend of Naomi's who'd enjoyed fondling her butt in public. I shrugged.

"Well, Joel remembers you. And he says he caught you checking out this chick on three separate occasions."

"What was he doing, stalking me?"

"Ha! You should talk."

I slung my book bag onto the kitchen table and marched over to the refrigerator. "Why are you even home right now?" I grumbled, surveying a plastic container full of leftover veggie lasagna. "Shouldn't you be out looking for a job?"

Naomi spat an olive pit at me.

She had a right to do so, I admit. The question had been a cheap shot. In truth, my sister had been looking for a job all summer—nine hours a day, six days a week, pretty much. But there were no jobs to be had. No good ones, anyway.

Naomi wanted to be a journalist. As far as Mom or Aunt Ruth or I could tell, she should have already been famous. Naomi Rosen wasn't just anyone. In June she'd graduated near the top of her class from the Columbia School of Journalism. This was after having been awarded a partial scholarship. Before that, she'd graduated *cum laude* from NYU after a scholarship *there*. But for some reason—because of the lousy economy, Naomi said—the only newspapers and magazines that were offering jobs were tabloids. She wanted to work for the *New Yorker*. She was even willing to start on a freelance basis, one story at a time.

So she was holding out.

And we supported her, of course. But after almost five months we were beginning to get nervous. Our eyes were already on the future. True, we'd always managed to survive on what Mom and Aunt Ruth make (they're both bookkeepers at Weber's: Mom is in charge of the apparel division; Aunt Ruth tallies up the home appliances sales), but all summer long we'd been counting on Naomi's dazzling new career to take off. I guess it was kind of like how some people count on winning the lotto, but with less risk. Once Naomi got a job, she would get her own place, and the rest of us would move uptown to a fabulous new apartment in a doorman/elevator building—because Naomi would be making so much money that she wouldn't know what to do with it all.

That was the plan, anyway.

"So what's this hot new senior chick's name?" Naomi asked.

I closed the refrigerator. "Olga Romanoff," I said.

She laughed.

"What?" I said.

"Nothing." She placed the jar of olives on the counter. Suddenly she smacked her forehead and closed her eyes. "Wait! Wait a second. I'm having a psychic experience. A revelation! Yes! An Italian name: Ravioli. No, Fettuccini. No . . . it's *Fanucci*. Celeste Fanucci."

I glared at her. "I thought you said you didn't know her name."

"I knew you'd never tell me the truth," she said. "So I was testing you via telepathic polygraph."

"Well, you better not say anything," I warned.

Naomi opened her eyes and smiled again. "Come on, Dave. How can I say anything? I don't even know her. Joel told me her name. Anyway, she's a kid. She goes to high school."

She said *kid* as if it were synonymous with *insect*.

"Whatever," I said. "Just don't say anything."

"Hey, man, I'm not the one who's stalking her."

"I'm serious. I know you'll talk to your butt-grabbing friend Joel, and *he'll* say something. Just try not to be a blabbermouth about this one thing, okay? Can you do that?"

Naomi sighed. "Joel hasn't grabbed my butt in over four years," she said. "And now that he's a teacher, he's Mr. Newbury to you. And who says *blabbermouth*?"

Before Naomi could go any further, the phone rang.

She dove for it. Her hip slammed into the table.

"*Ow!*" she yelped.

Normally I would have laughed. Not anymore. Now I felt bad. These phone freak-outs had become far too common. In the past two weeks alone, she had stubbed her toe, bruised her elbow, and banged her knee—all while racing to answer incoming calls. She still hadn't heard back from the *New Yorker* about her latest story idea: an investigation of organized crime in the recycling industry. She was pretty good about pretending to be optimistic ("Oh, I'm sure I'll get the gig any day now"), and even better at assuaging Mom and Aunt Ruth's doubts ("Everything takes time, you guys")—but her facade inevitably fell to pieces whenever the phone rang.

"Hello?" she gasped.

There was a brief pause. I looked at her, and then I looked at the floor. I didn't want to make her self-conscious.

She groaned.

"It's for you," she mumbled, thrusting the phone toward me. "Cheese."

* * *

My very first memory—I mean *ever,* as in all time—is of Greg "Cheese" Harrison standing in the foyer of our building refusing to wipe his nose.

It was winter. We were both four. His family had just moved into apartment 2F. Mom, Aunt Ruth, and I were on our way outside to play in the snow, and he was on his way in. He stood next to his father, bundled tightly in a hat, scarf, and mittens. All I recall seeing of his face were two red nostrils. One was completely crusted and stopped up, like the toilets at Yankee Stadium. The other ran as freely as a waterfall.

"Oh, you must be Mr. Harrison!" my aunt cried. "It's so nice to meet you!"

"So nice!" Mom added for good measure.

"Hello," said Mr. Harrison cautiously. He frowned at his son and shoved a tissue in his face. "Greg, wipe your nose," he commanded.

The kid didn't respond. He started twirling in circles. His hands remained at his sides.

As I hung shyly behind Mom and Aunt Ruth, bundled in my own bulky winter gear, I couldn't help feeling jealous. For one thing, this kid had a dad. Also, Mr. Harrison immediately started talking about how Greg was an only child. That meant he never got wedgies, or waited for the bathroom, or had a door slammed in his face. In other words, he lived in paradise. He was probably a huge brat. I remember hoping that I would never see him again. I also remember knowing that this wasn't going to be an option. He lived two floors below us.

Sure enough, after that first brief encounter Mom and Aunt Ruth kept up a nonstop rant about how nice it was going to be for me to have "a little buddy" in the building. We would probably end up being best friends forever, and wouldn't that just be wonderful!

They obviously didn't believe this. They were just looking for an excuse to get me out of the apartment for a few hours a week. But much to my surprise (and their eventual horror), they were right.

It started slowly at first: forced playtime in the park, awkward snack hours, that kind of thing. I learned that nobody called him Greg except his parents. He wouldn't even *answer* to Greg. He answered only to Cheese—the nickname his uncle had given him after he'd downed twenty-four slices of Swiss in one sitting and then proceeded to vomit for two straight days. I learned that he melted action figures in the microwave to create grotesque deformities, men with feet for heads or arms growing out of their chests. He tossed water balloons out his window. He built huge towers by gluing all his crayons together, and he encouraged me to do the same. He wanted a dog. He rarely sat still.

The more I learned, the more I liked.

A short time later we started going to the same school—PS 19, right down the block. We journeyed as a two-man unit from first grade to eighth grade. Along the way we discovered (among other things) pro wrestling, Sour Patch Kids, meatball heroes at Famous Ray's, the VH1 Classics network, those hole-in-the-wall CD shops on Mott Street, irony, *The Simpsons,* the Strokes, sneaking out of our building, girls, and that pro wrestling actually kind of sucked.

Then, without warning, Cheese's parents decided to send him to a private school in Greenwich Village.

We were both infuriated.

Everybody from PS 19 switched to Roosevelt in the ninth grade. *Everybody*. But there was nothing we could do. So three weeks before the beginning of freshman year, Cheese and I made a pact: we would treat high school like a job, the way adults treat work. You don't have *friends* at work. (Mom and Aunt Ruth certainly never socialize with the other people at Weber's.) You have colleagues, associates. You make polite chitchat with them during the day, you joke with them at the watercooler, and then you come home at night and hang out with your friends.

We shook on it.

All in all, the pact worked out pretty well—for me, at least. I found that it helped starting Roosevelt with a certain attitude, a philosophy. School was work. Fun was fun. I felt less lonely, even though I pretty much kept to myself.

Mom and Aunt Ruth must have been worried about me, though, because they bought me an electric guitar and amp for Hanukkah last year. There was no explanation. I hadn't asked for a guitar. I hadn't even hinted for one. The combo probably cost more than what they had spent on me for every previous Hanukkah combined. But, hey, maybe I actually *could* be the next Jimi Hendrix. They even gave me the exact same kind of guitar he played at Woodstock, a white Fender Stratocaster.

Unfortunately, in order to be a musician, I had to practice. I hated practicing. It hurt my fingers. But I did like hanging out with Cheese and trying to come up with band names. Cheese claimed that the Hanukkah gift was a sign: we *needed* to be rock stars. He was going to be the sexy, mercurial lead singer—like Julian Casablancas from the Strokes—and I was going to be the sullen, mysterious lead guitarist— like Jimmy Page from Led Zeppelin, before he got old and fat. Among our best names, or at least my favorites: Cajun Pimp Gumbo, House of Stank, the Mighty Tighty Whities, Fart Simpson, the Breath Penalty, and the Beatles: Part Deux.

We never had a rehearsal. And we never would. That's what made it so perfect. We were a band in names only.

True, not *everything* was perfect. A few things began to get on my nerves after Cheese switched to private school. Four, actually:

1. He started to say "dude."
2. He, too, would occasionally accuse me of not talking the way other guys talked.
3. He was making new friends, and I wasn't.
4. I was pretty sure he had the hots for my sister.

In the end, though, none of that stuff really mattered all that much. You don't stop shopping at your favorite bodega just because they move the candy dispensers to the rear. You simply make the extra effort to go get the Sour Patch Kids. But you always come back.

* * *

"Dude!" Cheese's voice boomed out of the earpiece. "So how was your second day of sophomore year?"

"Same old, same old," I said.

Naomi kept standing there after she handed me the phone, staring right at me. I grimaced. She rolled her eyes and marched out of the kitchen.

"Come on," Cheese prodded. "I want details."

I waited until I heard the sound of Naomi's bedroom door closing.

"There aren't any details," I said. I sat down at the kitchen table. "It's the same endless parade of baggy pants. The same aspiring wannabes, headed straight for the middle."

Cheese responded with an exaggerated sigh. "Jesus, Dave. You still sound like a weirdo. Why don't you try talking like your fellow man? Just for once?"

"I don't think it would do any good."

There was a click. Somebody had picked up on another extension. "Hello?" I said.

"Look, I'm expecting a call. Can you two wrap this up?"

It was Naomi, of course.

"We've only been on the phone for four seconds," I pointed out. "And we have call waiting, remember? My vocal cords do work. So if someone calls, I can just—"

"What's up, Naomi?" Cheese interrupted.

"Nothing. Did Dave tell you about the hot new senior chick he wants to bang?"

Cheese started cracking up.

"That's funny, Naomi," I growled. My face was suddenly on fire.

"Oh, *please,* Dave," she said. "If you want to bang Celeste Macaroni, you shouldn't stalk her. You should find out what her interests are. And if you discover that you share them, pursue them vigorously. Then talk to her."

"Aren't you expecting a call right now?" I asked.

Cheese snorted. "Dude, I can't believe you're stalking some senior chick," he said. "This is a new low."

"I'd say that *stalking* is a nice word for it, Cheese," Naomi stated gravely. Sarcasm dripped from her voice in great globs, like the snot from Cheese's nose that day we first met. "Frankly, I'm a little concerned. I'm telling you this because as Dave's friend, you have an obligation to help him. The massive shrine he built in Celeste Spaghetti's honor is particularly troubling. And last night I found him sleeping next to a mannequin-sized voodoo doll. It looked just like her."

"Well, what do you expect?" Cheese replied, as if they'd already had this same conversation dozens of times. "He has to do the whole shrine-and-voodoo-doll thing. What else can he do? Win her over with his charm and rugged good looks?"

"Bye, guys," I said.

"Wait!" Cheese yelled.

Naomi hung up first.

"Hello? Dave? You still there?"

"Yes, Cheese, I'm still here."

"Your sister's funny."

"So I've heard."

"She looks cool with her hair dyed black, too. I saw her the other day at—"

"Good-bye, Cheese." I hung up. If he wanted to continue the conversation, he could walk upstairs.

I sat there for a moment at the kitchen table. Something my sister had said stuck in my brain, even though I knew she hadn't been serious: *"You should find out what her interests are. And if you discover that you share them, pursue them vigorously. Then talk to her."*

Despite her brutal yet flowery language, the suggestion wasn't all that ridiculous. Why shouldn't I have some of the same interests as Celeste Fanucci? Maybe she liked Sour Patch Kids, too. Or coming up with silly band names. Or ragging on pro wrestling. The possibilities were infinite.

But how to find out these interests—that was the question.

I frowned. I already knew the answer. I would have to stalk her.

Chapter Three

I ended up stalking Celeste Fanucci for exactly two seconds.

On some level it was a relief because I felt creepy even *thinking* about it. As I walked to school the next morning I kept trying to come up with more pleasant ways of expressing the verb *stalk*. There was *spy,* but that was pretty creepy, too. *Eavesdrop* didn't do it for me, either. By the time I pushed through the heavy double doors of Roosevelt, I'd settled on *lurk*—as in, "to lurk near her, like that guy with the feather boa who used to lurk near our apartment building until the cops hauled him away." It wasn't much of an improvement.

My plan was to spend as much time as possible in the vicinity of my locker, with the hopes of maybe spotting her again randomly, as I had the day before. Her locker was only about twenty feet down the hall from mine. It was just close enough to catch a couple of snippets of conversation that might clue me in to her elusive "interests."

It wouldn't happen immediately; I knew that. I also knew that my plan was pathetic, if not criminal. But I tried not to dwell on the negatives. I tried to think about how patient I would be.

As it turned out, I didn't have to be patient at all.

The moment I rounded the corner, I practically ran into her. My feet screeched on the linoleum. I froze. I didn't know what to do.

She was wearing a frayed green dress with white polka dots. It had a homemade vibe. I imagined that her grandmother had stitched it.

On Olga Romanoff it would have looked like a shower curtain. On Celeste it looked like a ball gown.

She wasn't alone. She was talking to—of all people—Joel Newbury.

Joel's back was turned to me. I had no problem recognizing him, though, even from behind. He still had the same messy brown curls (a bigger, fluffier version of the hair on his chin) and the same slumped posture. He wore the same lame tweed jacket, too.

For the two seconds that I stood there like an idiot with my mouth hanging open, I wondered if he was stalking Celeste. Maybe it was an epidemic.

Celeste caught my gaze and smiled.

Joel glanced over his shoulder. "Well, well," he said, turning to greet me. "If it isn't young Master Rosen. What a coincidence."

Good Lord. He was sporting the air tie. That figured.

In case you don't know what the air tie is, it is unquestionably the worst fashion call ever to be made by a human being. And this is coming from somebody who normally doesn't give a crap about fashion. I have to be *provoked.* That's how bad it is.

The air tie is not an actual article of clothing. It is the phenomenon that occurs when somebody wears a collared dress shirt buttoned all the way to the top—*but with no tie.* In Cheese's words, "It is an affront to decent booty-shaking people everywhere." Generally, you see it on much-too-serious guys who wish they were successful artists, published poets, European, or the former managers of New Wave bands from the eighties. (Or, sadly, all of the above.) In Joel Newbury's case it made perfect sense.

"You've grown," Joel said. "To be a well-favored man is a gift of fortune."

"That's what they tell me," I said. I had no clue what he was talking about. He was probably quoting Shakespeare or something. I tried not to stare at Celeste.

"Celeste, this is Dave Rosen," Joel said. "He's the one I mentioned earlier."

My stomach lurched. *Naomi, you jerk.* I had a sudden, vivid fantasy of strangling my sister. I would wring her scrawny neck until her eyes popped out of her head. This was *not* cool. No, not cool at all . . . because the only possible reason Joel could have had for mentioning me earlier was that Naomi had told him to tell Celeste that I had a crush on her.

"Nice to meet you," Celeste said. She extended a hand.

"Uh . . . nice to meet you, too." I recovered long enough to shake it. Her fingers were tiny and soft. Everything about her was tiny and soft.

She and I were about the same height, I realized. In my thoughts she'd always towered over me by at least a few inches. And now that we were face to face, I also noticed that her eyes were very pale, sort of a translucent blue—and that if you looked long enough, you could detect a faint hint of gold, like the sky on a hazy fall morning.

In other words (and yes, I know this sounds horribly clichéd, but it's the *truth*), she was even more stunning and inaccessible-looking than I remembered.

I let go of her hand and looked down at my sneakers.

". . . would be happy to answer any questions about journalism," Joel was saying. Apparently he'd been talking the whole time. I hadn't noticed.

"Great!" Celeste exclaimed.

Joel patted me on the shoulder. "I should be getting to class. Great to see you, Dave."

"You, too, Joel," I lied.

"I'm afraid that's Mr. Newbury to you, now," he said.

I glanced up at him.

He smiled, but his eyebrows were raised. He fixed me with a meaningful stare. He wasn't joking.

"Right," I said. I kept my mouth shut after that. Odds were fairly good that if I opened it again, I would blurt out something offensive enough to get me suspended, or even expelled. I watched as he disappeared down the hall and into a classroom.

"He seems like a pretty cool guy," Celeste said.

"You might think differently if he used to knead your sister's ass in front of you."

Celeste giggled.

Blood rushed to my face. *Oops.* In my appalled state I'd forgotten where I was—and with whom. My eyes fell back to my sneakers.

"I guess there's some history between you two," she said. Her tone was dry, conspiratorial. She seemed to be hinting that she was already on my side. That didn't stop me from blushing, though. If anything, it made me blush worse.

"Well—uh—yeah—I mean not really," I stammered. "It's nothing. It's just that Joel—I mean, Mr. . . . (*What? Butt-Squeeze? Air Tie?*) . . . Joel went out with my sister, like, four years ago. For some reason they stayed friends after they broke up. Go figure."

Celeste laughed again. "I've never been able to figure that out," she said.

I tore my gaze away from the floor. "Huh?"

"I've never been able to figure out how two people stay friends after a breakup. I used to get asked that all the time. I always had to make something up."

"I'm sorry . . . I'm not following." I tried to smile.

She looked right at me. "No, I'm sorry. I should explain." Her demeanor suddenly became businesslike. "See, I started talking to Mr. Newbury because I found out that he helps run the school newspaper. Or he's going to, once it gets up and running this year. And since he's new, like me, I figured he might be more open to certain ideas than other teachers. See, I had this idea . . ." She rolled her eyes, as if embarrassed. "Okay, I'm rambling. Sorry! I wanted to write a story about real journalists. You know, about the real craft of investigative reporting, about finding human stories. And he said that he has a friend who's a real journalist—or is applying for a job as one—and that this friend has a little brother who's a student here. . . ." Her voice trailed off again. "You can probably fill in the blanks."

I can? All I had were blanks. She might as well have been speaking in Urdu. I was still trying to get over the miracle: *Here I am, talking to Celeste Fanucci. Here I am, taking my first steps across the unbridgeable chasm.* If only Jed Beck were present to bear witness. But why was this conversation even taking place? There were no celebrities in sight, no skeletons lumbering toward us. I had to get a grip. I could feel the clock ticking. Once again I was running late for Algebra II. I fought the urge to bolt.

Say something, Dave. You look like a fool. Say something.

"Are you some sort of couples therapist?" I asked.

I don't know why I said this. It was both moronic *and* totally deranged. (Have you ever heard of a seventeen-year-old couples therapist?) More importantly, it was in no way related to human stories, investigative reporting, the school paper, or Joel Rump-Grabber. It just popped out of my mouth, apropos of zilch—in the tradition of Grandpa Meyer. I guess it might have had something to do with the staying-friends-after-a-breakup comment she'd made. Maybe. But even then it didn't make much sense.

Celeste threw her head back and started cracking up.

So it seemed I was a comedian. Good. That was something.

Her laughter was pretty loud, in fact. And it didn't stop.

I cast a furtive glance in either direction. *Jesus.* Celeste Fanucci may have looked like a delicate green polka-dotted flower, but she laughed like an old drunk. She shrieked and cackled and stamped her Birkenstocks. A tear fell from her cheek.

Finally she managed to calm down.

"I'm sorry," she said. "It's just . . . Wow. You're pretty smart, you know that?"

I blinked. "I am?"

She took a deep breath and wiped her eyes. "No—I mean, yeah. It's just that my old principal once asked me the same thing. Only he said it in a much meaner way." She lowered her voice and scowled at me. "'Young lady, do you fancy yourself some kind of couples therapist?'" She paused. "Did Mr. Newbury tell you about my column?"

"Your . . . column?"

"I used to write an advice column for my old school newspaper," she said.

"Oh." I forced another clumsy smile. "You know, maybe you should start at the beginning. I'm a little lost."

The bell rang.

Celeste glanced at her watch, buried beneath a jumble of silver bangles and friendship bracelets. "Oh, man, I got art history right now," she said. She grinned apologetically and started backing away from me, toward the stairwell. "I'm sorry I'm such a total freak. Listen, I'll catch up with you later. It's . . . Gabe, right?"

"Dave," I said.

She rolled her eyes. "Ugh! I'm sorry, Dave! I'm a huge space case. Hey, you don't think your sister would mind if I called her today, do you? Mr. Newbury gave me her number."

I opened my mouth to say that no, of course Naomi wouldn't mind—but then I hesitated.

Naomi wouldn't mind, obviously. She'd probably be flattered. It might even take her mind off her crappy job situation for a while. But that wasn't really the point. The point was that she would probably use the call as an opportunity to tell Celeste that I wanted to "bang" her. Forget probably—she *definitely* would. And I couldn't allow that to happen.

So . . . *what?* I could make something up. Yes. I could tell Celeste that Naomi was out of town today, so Celeste should call her tomorrow. Perfect. That way I would have all night to convince Naomi (through a series of violent beatings) that she would end up at the bottom of the East River if she so much as *hinted* that I had a crush on Celeste.

Besides, I wasn't even sure if I had a crush on her anymore. Celeste was beautiful, even more beautiful than I'd suspected, but—by her own admission—she was also a "total freak" and a "huge space case."

On the other hand, the fact that she knew she was a total freak and a huge space case made her even more intriguing. . . .

Unfortunately, I never got the chance to lie about my sister's whereabouts. By the time I'd made my decision, Celeste had long since vanished up the stairs.

Chapter Four

I arrived home that afternoon to find Cheese sitting at the kitchen table with my sister, fiddling with my unplugged electric guitar. It sounded like torture. He was an even worse guitarist than I was. He wasn't a guitarist. (In all fairness, neither was I, really. But at least I owned a guitar.) I was surprised Naomi could take the racket. It made me think of a B-movie interrogation scene.

"Vee have vays of making you talk!"

"No! Please! Not the guitar stylings of Cheese! I'll tell you anything!"

Cheese's dark brown hair hung in his eyes. His hair always hung extra low these days; scruffy bangs were part of the hip new downtown image he'd been trying to cultivate. He was also wearing a black suit jacket—not because he had to, but because he thought it looked cool. His school didn't have a dress code. But they did have half-days on Wednesdays, which was why he'd beaten me home. He'd been done with classes since noon. Lucky jerk.

Naomi was eating olives again. The jar was almost empty. She looked pissed. But that might just have been because of Cheese.

Nobody said a word. Not even a "hey." I frowned. What was I, an apparition?

"Hello, New York!" I said. "Thanks for coming! I'd like to take this opportunity to send a special shout-out to the East Ninth Street Posse, for representing in full effect."

"Ha, ha, ha," Naomi grumbled.

Sometimes when my sister, Cheese, and I were in the same room—just the three of us—we conversed in what Cheese called "MTV Award Show Speak." Why, I'm not sure. It just sort of happened. I think Naomi started it. But we never did it in public, and it had nothing to do with how I didn't talk like other guys. It was a completely separate abnormality.

"What's the matter?" I asked. "Is something wrong?"

"A guy from the *New Yorker* called," Naomi said. "They passed on my story idea."

My shoulders sagged.

All day long I'd been rooting for her even more than usual—although I have to admit, it was mostly for selfish reasons. If she'd gotten the job, she would have left the apartment hours ago to chase down the gangsters of recycling. Which meant that she wouldn't have been around to take Celeste's call.

Then again, I didn't even know if Celeste had phoned yet. I hadn't seen her since our exchange of gibberish this morning.

"I'm sorry, Naomi," I said. I dropped my book bag on the floor and sat down.

She glared at the jar, as if it were somehow responsible for the bad news. "The guy said that my idea wasn't *edgy* enough. Since when has the mob stopped being edgy? Who the hell *makes* these decisions?"

"Screw the *New Yorker*," Cheese said. "Take it somewhere else."

"He also said I didn't have access to the right people, either," she muttered, reaching for the second-to-last olive. "I could have gotten access, though. He said I would have better luck pitching a story about a subject I know well—like 'youth culture,' or some other BS."

I bit my lip. "Hey . . . uh, can I ask you something?"

Naomi flashed me an evil smile. "Yes, Dave," she said. "I spoke to Celeste Fanucci."

"Oh." I could feel my stomach twisting, the blood pooling at my feet.

"She's quite a girl, Dave. Quite a girl." Naomi glanced over at Cheese. "Wouldn't you say so, Mac Daddy? You were here when she called."

Cheese didn't respond. He was bent over the guitar, lost in concentration. I detected an extremely off-kilter interpretation of "Row, Row, Row Your Boat" in the notes he was playing.

"Cheese?" Naomi said.

"What? Oh. Hey, I got a name for our first album." He looked up at me. *"The Mind Is a Terrible Thing."* He paused dramatically and grinned. "Huh? What do you think?"

Naomi frowned. "Cheese, you haven't started experimenting with drugs, have you?"

"The Mind Is a Terrible Thing," he repeated. He turned his attention back to the guitar. His hair fell over his face again, like the curtain at the end of a bad comedy skit.

"So . . . uh, what did you and Celeste talk about?" I asked Naomi, lamely attempting to sound casual.

Naomi's expression softened. "Don't worry; I didn't tell her that you have a crush on her." She sighed. "If you want to know, she was really cool. I feel bad for her."

My eyes narrowed. *Bad?* The word didn't compute. How could anybody possibly feel bad for the most prized member of the earth's most privileged species?

"I don't get it," I said.

"Well, she called to ask me what it was like to be a 'working journalist.' She wants to write a story about it. Not that I can even help, because I'm not a working journalist . . . *ugh.*" Naomi ran her hands through her messy black hair. "Anyway, when we were done, I asked her if she'd ever written for a school paper before. She started telling me about this advice column she used to write. It was kind of a 'Dear Abby' thing. 'Ask Celeste.' At first she wanted it to be really issues-oriented—you know, for kids to write in about race relations, or how they view the government, stuff like that. She wanted to spark debates and discussions. But after a while, everybody just ended up writing in about sex."

Cheese laughed. "Sex sells," he said.

Naomi glowered at him. He didn't notice. Now he was busy playing what sounded vaguely like the theme song from *Law & Order*, but out of tune and without rhythm.

"So she felt backed into a corner," Naomi went on. "The column was really popular. People from other schools even started writing in. On one hand, she didn't want to stop. She felt like people depended on her. But on the other hand, she felt kind of slimy. She felt like she was leading people on, pretending to be a Dr. Ruth type—when that wasn't what she wanted at all in the first place. She even changed the name of her column from 'Ask Celeste' to 'I'm No Expert.' Right after that, though, it got canned. She printed an anonymous letter where some girl asked if it was okay to occasionally have sex with an ex-boyfriend. Her principal almost suspended her."

Aha, I thought.

The conversation I'd had with Celeste earlier this morning was slowly emerging from the haze of pure nonsense. But there were still a few big pieces of the puzzle missing.

"So . . . ? Why do you feel bad for her? Because her column got canned?"

Naomi shook her head. She raised the olive jar and dumped the last olive into her mouth.

"I feel bad because she's lonely," she said, then chewed for a moment. "I mean, I was happy to talk to her, but I got the feeling she hadn't talked to anyone besides her parents in a really long time. She just moved here from L.A., so she doesn't know anybody. Plus, it's her senior year, so she's worried about college. She's trying to get involved in as many extracurricular activities as possible. She said, 'I need to figure out a fast way to make some new friends and fatten up my transcript—or I'll be in big trouble.' It was kind of sad, the way she said it. Sort of desperate."

I leaned back in my chair, stunned.

Wow. This was quite a revelation. I couldn't believe that Celeste Fanucci actually had real problems. She was too perfect for real problems. Plus, I'd always assumed that being a mysterious new transfer student would be exciting and novel—a way to reinvent oneself. But

I'd never imagined that it could be *lonely*. Not for somebody as perfect as Celeste.

"It's funny," Naomi added almost as an afterthought. "She told me that ever since she moved to New York she wishes *she* had an advice columnist."

"Really?" I said.

Naomi nodded. She grabbed the bowl of olive pits and dumped them into the garbage, then tossed the bowl into the sink and headed for the door.

Cheese abruptly stopped playing. "Hey, Naomi, why don't you write one?" he asked.

She turned. "Excuse me?"

"Why don't you write an advice column?"

She looked at him as if he'd just suggested that she rob a bank. "Why on earth would I ever want to do that?"

"Because you'd be good at it," he said. "Anyway, you were a psych major, right?"

"That doesn't make me a shrink, Cheese. I think you're giving me a little too much credit. I mean, look at how Dave turned out. My advice doesn't exactly pay off."

I smiled. "Bite me," I said. "Besides, when have I ever followed your advice?"

"No, I'm being serious," Cheese insisted. He brushed his bangs out of his eyes, nearly dropping the guitar. "You could even parlay it into a story about 'youth culture'—like that guy at the *New Yorker* said. I can already see the headline: 'Up-and-Coming Journalist Returns to High School Paper to Counsel Troubled Teens.'" He was wearing the same I'm-a-genius grin he'd worn moments ago, when sharing his brilliant idea for the name of our first album. "Huh? Huh? Now *that's* edgy. That's cash money in the bank. I'll take fifteen percent. And I'd just like to thank my Moms, my Pops, and God for making it all possible—and mostly, you, the fans."

Naomi laughed. "I pray for you, Cheese. I pray for your mental health."

"I mean it," he said.

"I'm sure you do." She turned and shuffled out of the kitchen. "And I appreciate the vote of confidence. In the meantime, you stay off those drugs, okay? Peace out."

Her bedroom door closed.

Cheese shook his head. "She doesn't understand me," he said. "Drugs are for the weak. I get high on life. And women. And rock 'n' roll. And occasionally bus fumes."

"And you say that I don't talk like my fellow man?" I mumbled.

"Yeah, but I keep my BS under wraps. That's the difference. Hey, dude, would it be cool if I borrow this until dinnertime?"

"Borrow what?" I asked.

"Your ax."

I laughed. "Why don't you just play it right here? I can stuff my ears with cotton and barricade myself in my room."

Cheese glanced up at me. "Can't I just borrow it until dinnertime?"

"Why? What's going on?"

"Well, it's just . . ." He squirmed a little, avoiding my eyes. "See, these guys at school are starting this band. You know, Darren and Mike? I told you about them. Anyway, Mike's guitar is in the shop. So I told him, you know . . ." He didn't finish.

I assumed that he was joking with me. "You told somebody I don't know that he could borrow my guitar?" I asked.

Cheese shrugged. "Yeah, well . . . I thought you'd be cool with it." He hid behind his bangs as he spoke. "I mean, this isn't like a joke band. It's real. Mike's a sick guitarist. I've heard him play. He wouldn't hurt it."

I frowned slightly. "You're being serious?"

"Yeah." Cheese tried to smile. "Come on, what's the big deal?"

"Uh . . . nothing," I said. "But just so you know, I let a guy at my school borrow your new laptop. He said he'd bring it right back. That's cool, right?"

"Whatever, dude," Cheese muttered. "You can come if you're so worried about it."

"Really? I can come? Gosh, you mean it?"

"Yeah," he said without a trace of humor.

"Well, that sounds great, Cheese," I stated as sarcastically as possible. "I can tag along with you and watch some sick guitarist named Mike play my guitar. Gee. Thanks."

Cheese pushed away from the table. His chair squeaked. He stood and handed the guitar to me with deliberate care, as if he were passing off a howling baby.

"Here you go, then, Dave," he said. "Here is your precious guitar. If I knew you cared about it so much, I wouldn't have touched it in the first place."

"You're *pissed* about this?" I asked, flabbergasted.

"No." He headed for the door. "I'll see you later."

I laughed again, even though I felt kind of queasy. Somehow, we were actually in a fight. Or close to being in one, anyway. I couldn't believe it. The last time we'd come close to getting into a fight was in March, when he'd forgotten my birthday. And I hadn't even really cared all that much. The only reason I ever remembered his birthday was because it was on Halloween.

"Whoa, hold up a sec," I called after him. "Where are you going?"

He paused in the front hall, where I could no longer see him. "To meet Darren and Mike."

I blinked a few times. "You're going to watch their band?"

"Well, I was going to try to be *in* their band," his disembodied voice replied. "But I guess I'll have to wait until Mike's guitar is fixed."

"I thought you said it wasn't a joke band."

"It's not."

Something wasn't quite connecting here. We might as well have been talking on crappy cell phones, because the signal—whatever the signal *was*—wasn't coming through. I was missing the meat of the conversation. "So what you're saying is . . ."

"Not everything has to be a joke, Dave," he grumbled. "I wanted to try to sing. Look, it's no big deal. I'll drop by later, all right?"

"Uh . . . sure."

The apartment door opened and closed. I heard the lock click back into place.

I swallowed.

The kitchen was silent. The guitar sat in my lap, digging into my thighs. I was half tempted to jump up and chase after him. But then I thought: *screw that.* If anything, *he* was the one who should come back and apologize to *me.* I was actually sort of mad. Who the hell did Cheese think he was, offering my "ax" to a stranger—or even trying to be in a nonjoke band at all? He couldn't *sing.* That was the whole point. That was what made our phony musical aspirations *funny.* He couldn't sing, and I couldn't play.

But that wasn't the truly heinous part. No, the truly heinous part was that by going to meet these guys, he was dishonoring our pact to treat school as work. He might as well have been joining the company volleyball team or something. It was ridiculous. It was *wrong.*

So if Cheese wanted to do the *right* thing, he would come back.

Somehow, though, I had a feeling he wouldn't. Not soon, anyway. Probably not until after dinner, when Mom and Aunt Ruth served up the organic chocolate-chip cookies that Cheese's parents refused to stock at home.

Which meant that for the first time in a long while, I had the entire evening to myself.

Which was fine.

No, it was *better* than fine. It was a great opportunity.

I was free for once. I could do my homework, watch TV, surf the Net, read a book, bug my sister . . . maybe even practice guitar.

There was only one drawback.

I realized right away that freedom sucked.

Chapter Five

The idea came to me that night during dessert. Or at least the *seed* of the idea came to me. I'm not sure exactly why, either. Maybe it was because I was bored and lonely. Maybe it was because I was pissed at Cheese, who still hadn't called or dropped by to apologize. Or maybe it was because Naomi wouldn't shut up about how Mom and Aunt Ruth had finally gone off the deep end by buying Woodstock Freddy's Healthy All-Natural Brownies! (With an exclamation point.) They tasted like cement mix.

Yes, that was the clincher: the new brownies, plus the sound of Naomi's angry voice, combined with my general misery and the relentless beat of Sly and the Family Stone's "Hot Fun in the Summertime"—which Mom and Aunt Ruth had slipped into the CD player *again,* for the second night in a row. . . . I snapped. I needed something to *do* with myself. Immediately. I had to take my mind off the real world. Or at least "Woodstock Freddy."

"Listen, Naomi," I said. "Can you drop the dessert rant for a second?"

She scowled at her half-eaten brownie. "Why? This is important."

"Because I have a question."

"What is it?"

"Do you think Joel Newbury would let me write an advice column for the school paper?"

"What?" She raised her eyes and smiled at Mom and Aunt Ruth. "You hear that? Ha!"

They both moaned.

Just so you know, Mom and Aunt Ruth moan all the time. The sound they make is deep and gravelly, like Marge's sisters on *The Simpsons*—to whom Cheese once compared them, in fact. But it has nothing to do with how they feel. It's just a reaction, almost a nervous tic.

(A quick note: If you're unfamiliar with *The Simpsons*, Marge's sisters also happen to be old, unmarried twins who share an apartment and work at the same place. And they are slightly overweight. So I admit, there are some similarities. However, I feel it's important to point out that Cheese later felt sorry about making the comparison. Marge's sisters are cruel blue-haired hags. They smoke. Mom and Aunt Ruth have gray hair, and they haven't smoked in years. And they are very hospitable. They ply Cheese with health food and free access to our apartment, even though they've told me numerous times that he's a weirdo and that I should make new friends.)

"Come on, Dave," Naomi said gently. "Maybe you should give this Celeste Fanucci thing a rest. I'm sure there are plenty of cute girls in your own class who have crushes on you."

"Who's Celeste Fanucci?" Mom asked. She began to clear the table.

"Nobody," I said. "And this has nothing to do with her, anyway."

Aunt Ruth patted my head. "It's okay to have a crush on someone older. It's natural."

"I'm sure it is. But like I said, this has—"

"Remember Saul Weinberg?" Aunt Ruth interrupted. She turned and waggled her eyebrows at my mother. "You might as well have held that boy on a leash, the way he followed you around. Remember that?"

"That wasn't me, that was you," Mom replied. She pulled on a pair of yellow dishwashing gloves and turned on the faucet. Steam began to rise from the sink. "Saul Weinberg liked *you.*"

Aunt Ruth shook her head. "No, the boy who liked me was Peter . . .

Peter Brown. Peter *something*. Short little squirt. He had that limp, you know—and the condition with his teeth. Saul was handsome. I hear he's a nutritionist now. You always got the handsome ones."

"Please," Mom said. "Saul was nothing special. And Peter Brown's teeth were fine. They were just yellow. Dave, it's your turn to dry the dishes tonight."

"The boy needed a dentist," Aunt Ruth said.

"The boy needed to quit smoking reefer," Mom said. "That was the problem. Fourteen years old, and he smoked reefer the way most children chew gum. It stained the enamel." She began to scrub the plates. They clinked as she placed them in the drainer. "Dave? A little help?"

"Everybody smoked reefer back then," Aunt Ruth said. "It was a different time."

"Maybe, but Peter Brown was a walking smokestack. A *limping* smokestack."

Aunt Ruth sniffed. "So what are you saying? That the only reason this poor cripple had a crush on me was because he was too high to know any better?"

"Oh, come on, Ruth. Why do you always sell yourself short?" Mom frowned at me over her shoulder. "Dave? Can you get off your posterior and help already?"

I shot Naomi a stony glance: *Make up something to get me out of here. You got them started. You owe me one.*

She smirked.

"You guys, is it all right if Dave doesn't dry the dishes tonight?" she asked. "He needs me to help him with his algebra homework, and there's a documentary I want to watch later."

Mom and Aunt Ruth moaned.

For somebody who is so terrible at keeping secrets, Naomi is also a very convincing liar. It's a dangerous combination.

"Thanks, you guys," I said. "I'll dry the dishes tomorrow night, I promise."

Neither Mom nor Aunt Ruth protested. Maybe they'd run out of the energy needed to form actual words. Naomi and I jumped up and dashed down the hall to her room.

I slammed the door behind us, muffling the sounds of Sly and the Family Stone.

"Sorry about that," Naomi muttered. She laughed and flopped down on her unmade bed. "Honestly, I didn't mean to send them off on a trip down memory lane."

"Yeah, well . . ." I was about to point out that *everything* sends them down memory lane (a fact Naomi knew very well)—and worse, she had implanted Celeste Fanucci's name in their brains for all time, so they would probably hound me about her until I was old enough to collect social security. But I didn't. I glanced around the room instead. *Jeez.* It looked as if it had been ransacked. Clothes and books were strewn everywhere; drawers were flung open; a bra hung precariously across her computer screen. Her desk was buried beneath several layers of crumpled newspaper. It was a little disturbing. Generally Naomi was sort of a neat freak.

"What?" Naomi said.

"Uh, nothing. Is everything all right?"

"Yeah. Why?"

"I don't know. Your room—"

"Look, I'm a little busy these days, all right?" Naomi snapped. She fluffed a pillow and leaned against it. "I don't have time to dust and vacuum every afternoon."

I didn't know what to say. I grabbed a pile of notebooks off the desk chair and moved them to the floor, then sat down.

"I'm sure you'll get a job soon," I told her.

Naomi sighed. "I know. I know." She shook her head and mustered a tired smile. "Look, I'm sorry. Let's not talk about it. It's too depressing. Let's talk about this demented scheme of yours to win the affections of Celeste Fanucci."

"I *told* you," I said. "This has nothing to do with her."

"So you're telling me that you suddenly want to write an advice column—even though an advice column is something you've never mentioned, much less *read*, in your life—and it has nothing to do with the fact that Celeste used to write one."

I laughed in spite of myself. "Okay, maybe a little. But it doesn't have anything to do with wanting to win her affections. It just sounds like a cool thing to do."

"You're talking to *me*, Dave," Naomi said. "Remember? So drop the BS. I know what's going on. You're hoping that if you write an advice column, Celeste will write in. Then you're hoping that some kind of wonderful romance will blossom from it—because you'll offer her the most amazing words of wisdom—and after that, you'll get married and have a hundred kids, and Lifetime will make a movie out of it."

"Gee, how did you know?" I said flatly.

"I'm being serious," she said.

"Me too. But I'm not sure about Lifetime. I was thinking the Hallmark channel. I hear they pay more."

I was actually a little annoyed. But that was probably just because there was a big kernel of truth to what Naomi was saying. The problem was, I hadn't allowed myself to think about it in such stark and pitiful terms. But yes, now that it was out in the open, I guess I *had* been secretly hoping to forge some kind of relationship with Celeste Fanucci. Maybe I could somehow get her to write in and share all her problems with me. I could help her feel less lonely. Plus I could learn about all of her interests. And we would become kindred advice-columnist spirits. It worked on so many levels.

Naomi looked me in the eye. "So you're saying that you just want to write an advice column for the hell of it."

I blinked. "That's what I'm saying. Well, sort of. It's just . . . I need something to *do*. I'm bored. And if you talk to Joel Newbury about it, I bet he'd let me do it. Of course, you might have to let him grab your butt a few times—"

Naomi hurled her pillow at me.

I ducked. It smashed into the wall and knocked her calendar to the floor, then landed on her computer.

"Dave, I'm all for you getting involved with the school newspaper," she said seriously. "I mean it. I think it's a good idea, and you'll meet new people. Celeste included. But maybe you should go about it in a different way."

"But what's wrong with *this* way?" I said. "Maybe I can actually help people."

"Dave, come on." She flashed me that I'm-your-older-sister-so-I-have-infinite-wisdom smile. I hated when she did that. "Guys don't write advice columns. Women do."

"Yeah, but I'm not like other guys. Everybody says so. Everybody says I talk funny. So maybe I'll bring something new to the table, something totally different. I mean, women play pro basketball, right? So why can't men write advice columns?"

Naomi slumped back on her mattress. "Fine. I'll tell you what. I'll ask you a question right now, and you go write an advice column about it. And if I think it's good, I'll talk to Joel."

I frowned at her. I knew this was probably a trap, but somehow it sounded perfectly easy. "Really? You swear?"

"Yeah, but you have to do it right now."

"Fine. What's the question?"

Naomi sat up straight again. "Dear Mr. Advice Columnist. My little brother has been driving me insane with this crush he has on an older girl. He seems to have lost touch with reality. What should I do? Sincerely, Ms. Fed Up."

Ha, ha, ha, I thought.

So I was a sucker. Not that this was anything new. I should have known better. But I refused to let my sister win so easily. I was fed up, too—not with her, necessarily, but with life in general. If she wanted to play it that way, I could play it that way myself. She'd set the terms. Which meant that if I did a good job, she would have to honor her end of the bargain.

"No problem," I said. "I'll be right back."

* * *

Forty-five minutes and three drafts later, I knocked on Naomi's door. Aunt Ruth and Mom were still in the kitchen. They peered down the hall at me.

"Yeah?" Naomi called.

"My algebra homework is done," I replied. "Can you look at it?"

Naomi chuckled. "Sure. No problem."

The door opened. I stepped inside, then sat down at the desk and shoved this piece of paper into Naomi's hands:

Dear Ms. Fed Up,

I understand your annoyance. Believe me. It's difficult when family members can't see the truth about their own lives, even when the truth is smacking them over the head with a two-by-four. Part of us feels sorry for them. The other part is just angry. It's doubly annoying when they won't shut up about it.

On the other hand, try to put yourself in his shoes. Have you ever had a crush on somebody? (If you haven't, you've got bigger problems than your brother.)

The point is that everybody has crushes. It's natural. It's part of growing up. The best thing to do is to let your little brother's crush run its course. Obviously, dissuade him from stalking this girl or getting creepy with her. But don't make him feel as though he's different or weird, either.

Some people crush harder than others. The people close to them may have a hard time understanding this. Eventually, though, your little brother will grow out of his crush and move on.

And I know he may get on your nerves, but here's
something you might also want to think about: I'll
guarantee you that somebody somewhere has had a crush
on you at some point in your life. You may even have
noticed it. And I'll bet that made you feel pretty
good. Flattered, even. Which is probably how the girl
your little brother likes is feeling right now. And
in this crazy world we live in, it's always a good
thing when somebody feels good, right?

Sincerely,
Mr. Advice Columnist

Naomi's face didn't register any reaction. She read it a second
time, then a third.

"If it sucks, just tell me," I muttered.

"No." She shook her head and blinked, as if she'd just woken up
from a nap. "It's not that. It's, ah . . . it's really good."

I frowned at her. "It is?"

She sat down on the edge of the bed. "Yeah." Her eyes roved over
the page again. "I mean, some of the wording is a little awkward, and
it's a little too long, but all in all . . ." She glanced up at me. "How did
you come up with this stuff?"

I shrugged. "They say that if you live in France long enough, you
eventually learn how to speak French."

"What's that supposed to mean?"

"It means that I've lived with neurotic, high-strung, over-
analytical chicks my entire life. Something's bound to rub off."

A smile spread across her face. She nodded, impressed. "Point
well taken," she said.

"So you'll talk to Joel?" I asked.

"I will talk to Joel, Mr. Advice Columnist. I most certainly will."

Chapter Six ▬▬▬▬▬▬▬▬▬

The problem with having a life-altering mission when you go to school is that it takes over your brain completely, so you can't concentrate. It gets worse when your first period is Algebra II. It gets even worse than *that* when your teacher is Mr. Cooper—a man so stiff, formal, and mean-spirited he makes you feel as if you've been magically transported to some crusty boarding school, like the kind you see lampooned in those ancient hair-metal videos on VH1 Classics. (*"What's this? A Mötley Crüe sticker in your lesson book! That's forty lashes!"* Not that he would say those exact words, per se. But close.) You start to wonder why you even bothered to show up at all.

In a way, though, I really *didn't* show up to Algebra II the next morning. Sure, my body was there. But my mind was off in a glorious and not-too-distant future, sharing a bag of Sour Patch Kids with Celeste Fanucci:

CELESTE: *I don't know how you did it, Dave.*
ME: *Did what?*
CELESTE: *How you understood me so perfectly, just from the way I phrased a simple question. I mean, you knew that I was secretly in love with you. And all I wrote was: "Dear Mr. Advice Columnist, Can a senior girl ever bridge the unbridgeable chasm with a sophomore boy?" How did you figure it out?*

ME: (I shrug.) *Wisdom and intuition, I guess. And the fact that I don't talk like other guys. Hey, do you mind if I have that last cherry Sour Patch Kid?*

CELESTE: *Here, have the whole bag.* (She hands me the bag and looks me in the eye. The gesture speaks volumes.) *Dave, will you run away with me?*

ME: *Hmm.* (I casually finish the last cherry Sour Patch Kid.) *Running away is never the answer, Celeste. As advice columnists, we both know that. But in this case, I'll make an exception. Where to?*

Okay. Maybe the not-too-distant future wouldn't be quite that glorious. It all depended on Joel Newbury. If he liked my sample column as much as Naomi did (or claimed she did), great. But even then, I still had to convince him that such a column would be worthy of the school paper. And if he didn't like it . . . Well, no, it was best not to obsess about the what-ifs. I simply had to have Faith.

Naomi had faxed the column to Joel first thing this morning—along with a note she wouldn't let me read, even though I'd banged on her locked door so many times that Mom and Aunt Ruth swore they'd toss me out with the recycling, to be hauled away by "those Mafia hoodlums your sister keeps carrying on about." So I was a little anxious. I hadn't seen him yet. I kept rehearsing our conversation in my head. (That is, when I wasn't having shameful fantasies about running away with Celeste Fanucci.) I would call him Mr. Newbury. I would even try to ignore the air tie.

On the other hand, I did have some Hope. Because late the night before a funny thought had occurred to me. . . .

He still has the hots for Naomi, doesn't he?

Of course he did. Why else would he make it a point to stay friends with her? After all, Celeste Fanucci herself—veteran advice columnist and reluctant "couples therapist"—could never figure out why exes remained friends after a breakup. The way I saw it, Joel must have never wanted to break up with Naomi in the first place. (I was pretty sure *he* had broken up with *her*, although why she'd agreed to go out with him in the first place was anyone's guess.) So maybe he would do me this favor, as a way to get back in good with—

"Dave!"

I blinked.

Mr. Cooper was staring at me from the head of the classroom. He didn't look pleased. I could actually see his craggy face darkening like a movie theater right before previews.

"What is the variable in this equation?" he snapped.

"The . . . variable?"

A couple of kids giggled.

"Yes, David," he said slowly. "The *variable*? The unknown factor? You do know what that is, don't you?"

I nodded, staring right back at him. I was pretty sure I knew what the variable was. Unfortunately for me, it had nothing to do with the problem on the chalkboard. It had to do with the pretentious schmuck who'd once enjoyed fondling my sister's butt in public.

* * *

"Young Master Rosen!"

When I first heard Joel's voice booming down the hall right before second period, I cringed. It was instinct, I guess. But then I remembered: I was looking for him. Right. So this was a stroke of luck. I pasted a big fat phony smile on my face and turned to wave.

My mouth fell open.

What the—

Okay. Something very strange was going on.

Joel Newbury was unrecognizable. It was definitely him, though, because he was walking straight toward me. The goatee was gone. So was the scraggly hair. So was the air tie. (Thank God for that, at least.) Joel Newbury was *bald*—or clean-shaven, anyway. He was wearing a black turtleneck. And a black leather jacket. And horn-rimmed glasses. I didn't even know he *needed* glasses. In short, he'd gotten a complete makeover. Now he looked like one of those hipster/nerds who play weird outlaws in low-budget independent films.

"I've been getting that all morning," he said.

"Getting what?" I asked, still in shock.

"That rude look," he answered dryly.

Whoops. I shook my head and forced a laugh. "Oh! Sorry! I mean, no, you know, it's just . . . ah, you sort of took me by surprise there, Jo— Mr. Newbury."

"Yes. Well, change is good, as they say." He smiled. "Nothing is permanent but change."

I nodded, resisting the urge to run. "Sure. Absolutely."

"I've been looking for you," he said.

"Really?" I laughed again. For some reason this made me nervous.

"Yes . . . listen." He paused and glanced around the deserted hallway. Second period had begun, which meant I was late for study hall. "I'd like to talk to you for a minute," he said.

I shrugged. "I . . . uh, well, I'd like to talk to you, too, but I have study hall right now—"

"I'll write you a note," he interrupted.

Hmm. Getting reacquainted with old Mr. Newbury could be more useful than I'd imagined. "What's up?" I asked.

"You know, I'm not even sure," he said in an oddly distant voice. He leaned toward me. "I'm a little concerned about your sister," he whispered.

I frowned. "Why? What happened?"

"I just got off the phone with her." He glanced around once more to make certain we were alone. "I'm worried about her job situation."

I didn't answer. I was worried about her job situation, too, of course. But I wasn't sure if it was Joel Newbury's place to be worried about it as well.

"This is an awkward thing, Dave," he went on. He lowered his eyes. "You see, earlier this morning she faxed me . . . an article. Did she tell you anything about it?"

I laughed. "Yeah, I—"

"Did she tell you to tell me that *you* wrote it?" he demanded, suddenly staring right at me.

I shook my head, baffled. "What do you mean? I *did* write—"

"Listen, Dave," he interrupted. "I don't want to get excessively personal. I know it's not appropriate for me to pry into your family matters. On the other hand, I am an old friend of your sister's, and this is an issue that concerns not only me but the school." His face softened. "I'm sorry. I don't mean to be so melodramatic, either. It's just . . . if your sister wants to write an advice column for the school paper, that's fine. I won't think any less of her. I won't think she's a failure because she's not writing for the *New Yorker.* In fact, I think it's a wonderful idea. But she doesn't have to put on this elaborate charade. Just tell her that, okay? I'd be very grateful."

I stood there.

Whoa.

If I'd understood him correctly . . . I started to smile. This was unbelievable. No, *unbelievable* wasn't a strong enough word. This made his bizarre new hairless getup seem like nothing.

"So let me get this straight," I finally said. "You think that Naomi wrote the column?"

"I know that Naomi wrote the column, Dave."

I burst out laughing.

Unfortunately, Joel didn't seem to think any of this was funny. "I'm just curious," he said, sounding annoyed. "What is she up to? Is this some sort of angle for a story she's pitching? Is that why she needs your cooperation? Or is she just playing a practical joke on me?"

"No, Jo— I mean, no." I shook my head. "It's no joke."

"Well, good," he said. "Because I already mentioned this to some people in the administration, and they agreed: it would be great for a bright young alumna like Naomi to offer advice to students in a public forum. If it's tastefully done, that is. I think kids would really go for it. And the fact that she's a journalist and a psych major . . . It could be really terrific. I tried to tell her all this on the phone just now. But she wouldn't hear it. She wouldn't drop this ridiculous story about how she's trying to help you get a 'gig' writing for the school paper."

He enunciated the word *gig* to make it clear that he was using Naomi's word, not his. Not that I would have thought otherwise.

"So will you please just tell her that if she wants to write this column, she's welcome to?"

I bit my lip. I was having a hard time not breaking into hysterics.

"All she has to do is call," he said curtly. "I'll make the arrangements." He raised an eyebrow. "Look, I understand that you're loyal to your sister. I admire that. Just please pass on this message for me, okay? Thanks. I appreciate it." He turned to leave.

"Wait! Can I ask you something?"

"What, Dave?"

"How come you're so sure Naomi wrote the column?"

He paused. At first I thought he was mad. But then he grinned over his shoulder. His brand-new leather jacket creaked. Something in his smile made me think of a young dad whose toddler had asked an incredibly inane question—like *"Daddy, does Santa ever stop to go poo-poo at our house?"* He might as well have been saying, *"Aw . . . aren't you cute. You're so incredibly ignorant."* I wanted to punch him in the face.

"I'm sure you're a fine writer, Dave," he said. "But I know your sister. She's got a certain way of thinking . . . a feminine way of thinking. We men just don't write like that—no matter how talented or mature we may be." He chuckled. "Speaking of which, I'll take care of that note for study hall right now, all right?" He winked. "I'll be sure to write a good one."

Chapter Seven

The rest of the day passed in a dark fog. If concentration had been difficult *before* that jarring little encounter with Joel, now it was impossible. I barely even noticed Celeste, even though she said hi to me in the halls four different times. (Okay, "barely" is an exaggeration.) My brain was like a merry-go-round. One second I'd feel amused; the next, offended; the next, I didn't know what. In the end I mostly felt nauseated. Not only did I not talk like other guys, I didn't write like them, either. Apparently my writing was "feminine." What the hell did that *mean*? More importantly, what would Celeste think? What was going on here?

By the time I got home, I was actually a little pissed off. This was all Naomi's fault. It was up to her to fix the problem. As soon as I walked into the apartment, I marched right to her room and banged on her door. I didn't even bother to take off my book bag.

"Dave?" she said.

"That's not what Joel thinks," I stated.

Naomi opened up and offered a sheepish smile.

Yikes. For a second I forgot about being angry. She was a mess. She was still wearing her pajamas. Her hair stuck straight up, as if she'd been electrocuted. I peered into her room. The shades were drawn. Her flickering monitor was half buried in newspaper, and the debris seemed to explode outward from there—onto the floor in spiraling arcs of wadded napkins and diet-soda cans. (The whole scene vaguely reminded me of *Fat Albert,* the seventies cartoon about a bunch of groovy kids who hang out in a junkyard, and whose episodes never fail to send Mom and Aunt Ruth into hysterics.) Naomi had probably been holed up here all day. Maybe Joel was right to be worried about her. Maybe I should have been more worried.

"Listen, Dave, I . . ." She giggled, then quickly clamped her hand over her mouth. "Sorry. Come in."

"Are you all right?" I asked.

"Yes, *Mom,* I'm fine," she muttered. "Tell me what happened."

I shrugged. "There isn't much to tell," I said, dumping my book bag on top of a pile of dirty laundry. I sat on the edge of her bed. "Joel thinks you wrote the column."

She nodded. Her lips twitched. She was doing her best not to laugh.

Now I wasn't so worried about her anymore. Now I wanted to punch *her* in the face.

"I know. . . . He told me the same thing," she finally managed. "It's crazy. What did he say to you?"

I shrugged. "Basically that I *couldn't* have written the column, because we men aren't that 'feminine.' Oh—and that change is good. 'Nothing is permanent but change,' he said. That's an exact quote."

Naomi's forehead wrinkled. "Why did he say that?"

"Because he came to school bald."

"He came to school—*what?*"

"He shaved his head and his beard. And he was dressed all in black. He had weird glasses, too—you know, the ones that are ugly and expensive." I rubbed my eyes, suddenly exhausted for some reason. "Maybe he's hosting a poetry slam. Or he's becoming a Buddhist."

Naomi didn't say anything. I glanced up at her. She was staring off into space, just the way Grandpa Meyer used to do before one of his sneezing fits. All at once she started to giggle again.

"Oh, my God," she murmured.

"What?"

"I don't believe it," she said. She sat down at her desk. "See, he and I got into this fight on the phone the other day . . . well, it wasn't a fight, really. It was more of a joke fight. But I told him that if he wanted to win the respect of his students, he had to update his image. He had to stop dressing like Jerry Seinfeld, circa 1990, unless he was actively seeking a lifetime of abuse. And he said that he—" She broke off, staring at me. "What?"

"Nothing. This is a truly fascinating story. Please, do go on."

She smirked. "Come on. It's just . . . you've seen him. I mean, think of how a guy like Cheese would rag on him. There must be a hundred wiseasses like Cheese at Roosevelt. Think of the torture he would endure on a daily basis." She laughed again. "But I guess he finally came to his senses. You say he was dressed all in black?"

I nodded. In all honesty, though, I'd pretty much forgotten what we were talking about. Because the moment she mentioned Cheese, I felt an unpleasant knot in my stomach.

"Um . . . did Cheese call or stop by today?" I asked.

Naomi furrowed her brow. "No," she said. "Why? What does that have to do with Joel's wardrobe?"

"Nothing," I said. My throat tightened. I wasn't sure why, but I was pissed off at Naomi again. I didn't want to talk about Joel Newbury or his stupid new wardrobe. I wanted to tell her that there *weren't* a hundred wiseasses like Cheese at Roosevelt. There were *no* wiseasses like Cheese at Roosevelt. There were only meatheads like Jed Beck, which was why it sucked. In fact, when I really thought about it, the closest thing I had to a buddy at that lame school—even on the lowest, job-only, watercooler level—was Joel Newbury himself. And that wasn't just pathetic, it was horrifying.

"Hey, is something wrong, Dave?" Naomi asked.

"Yeah, something's wrong. Your ex-boyfriend thinks *you* wrote what *I* wrote."

"Besides that, I mean."

"No," I lied. I pushed myself off the mattress and stood. "Listen, just make sure Butt Man knows the truth, okay? Can you please do that for me? This is ridiculous."

"I *know* it's ridiculous!" she yelled, laughing. "I must have called him five times today already. That's the whole point, Dave. He won't listen. He thinks I'm playing some weird mind game. But, hey, you should take it as a compliment. It's a testament to how good an advice columnist you are."

I rolled my eyes. *Please.* That was garbage, and Naomi knew it. Did she honestly think it would make me feel better? It made me feel *worse.* It made me feel sick. Hooray for me! I was such a good advice columnist that Joel Newbury thought I was my sister.

"Listen, Dave. Sit down for a second," Naomi said seriously. "I want to throw out an idea at you. I've been thinking about it all day. It's sort of wacked, though."

"What, you've decided to wash your hair?"

"Ha, ha," she said. "Just sit down."

I sighed. I knew that if I left, I would probably just go and sulk in my room. It wasn't as if I would march down to Cheese's apartment and demand to know why he'd suddenly decided to blow me off just because of some petty little nonargument. (Besides, it was up to *him* to come apologize to *me.*) It wasn't as if I would do any Algebra II homework, either. Nope. Once again, I was totally free. *Free*—my favorite four-letter *F* word. I plopped back down on Naomi's bed.

"All right," she said. "Don't interrupt or say anything until I'm done, okay?"

I yawned loudly.

She smiled. "And try not to be a little jerk, either."

"You're littler than I am, if you want to get technical. You're barely three-dimensional."

"And you're Mr. Universe," she said dryly. "Listen, remember what Cheese said yesterday?"

"'*The Mind Is a Terrible Thing.*'"

"Dave!" she barked.

"You asked me what he said."

"It was a rhetorical question." She scooted forward on the chair. "He said that I should write an advice column because I could parlay it into a story about youth culture. And I know that he was just being a comedian, the way he always is. But after what happened today with Joel, I started thinking. He might have been on to something."

I sat up straight. *On to something?*

Now she had my attention. Less than twenty-four hours ago this very same idea had prompted her to ask Cheese if he was on drugs.

"What if we pretended that I *did* write the column?" Naomi continued. "Because that way you and I would both get what we want. So would Joel. He'd get his column written by 'me.' And since you'd do the actual *writing,* you'd get to help your schoolmates—like this girl you're so into, Celeste Fanucci. I mean, you'd actually make a difference in her life. And I'd get to develop a cool pitch for a story: 'Young Journalist-slash-Psych-Major Revisits High School to Counsel Troubled Teens,' or whatever it was Cheese said." She grinned, looking like a demented infomercial hostess. "See? We can't lose!"

I swallowed.

"What?" she said.

She must have been joking. I *prayed* she was joking. "You need to get out of the apartment more often," I said. "You're going a little bonkers."

"Come on, Dave," she groaned. "I'm serious. And who says *bonkers?*"

"You honestly don't think we could get away with—"

"We already have gotten away with it!" she interrupted.

I opened my mouth to argue, then stopped.

She was right. Not only had we already gotten away with it, we couldn't seem to talk our way out of it. As far as Joel was concerned, Naomi had written the column. Period. And nothing, apparently, could change his mind.

"I'll help you with the whole thing," she went on, capitalizing on my lost momentum. "I'll help you sort through the questions. I'll help you pick the best ones and edit your responses. Not that you need much editing. I mean, I sent Joel exactly what you wrote, word for word."

I frowned. She was trying to butter me up again. She wasn't very good at it. She hadn't had a whole lot of practice.

"I mean it, Dave," she said. She lowered her voice to a whisper and smiled at me, leaning so far forward on the chair that I thought she might fall off. Her dark eyes twinkled in the fluorescent glow of the computer monitor. "It could be a lot of fun."

"Yeah, but . . ."

"But what?"

I chewed my lip.

My sister had come up with a lot of insane schemes over the years. Especially in *recent* years. Like two summers ago, when she somehow convinced Mom and Aunt Ruth to join something called the Men's Hair Society. She figured it would be a great way for them to meet virile, if balding, bachelors. Poor Mom and Aunt Ruth called a 1-800 number and were charged over fifty bucks apiece in nonrefundable application fees before the automated Hair Line determined that they were, in fact, women, and therefore ineligible for membership. (It probably didn't help that they weren't interested in wigs or transplants, either.) They never got the name of a single bachelor.

Then there was the time last spring when Naomi nearly talked Cheese into stealing his parents' SUV. She claimed she had to take pictures of him behind the wheel for her graduate thesis, something about the "excesses of urban youth." At the time, Cheese had never operated a motorized vehicle other than a model airplane. (As far as I know, he still hasn't.) "Driving isn't all that hard," Naomi kept telling him—as if she had any clue, which she didn't, because as a lifelong New Yorker, she'd never bothered to get a license. "We'll just go for a quick spin around the block." Luckily, neither she nor Cheese could figure out how to start the engine.

In short, I knew that all of Naomi's insane schemes had one thing in common: they all ended in catastrophe. (Or they would if they ever got off the ground in the first place.)

On the other hand, I also knew she needed something to *do* with herself—something to make her feel productive, to bring her closer to that elusive gig that would change all our lives for the better . . . even if it involved perpetrating a fraud on her former boyfriend.

I could probably use something to do with myself, too. I wasn't exactly a Polaroid of contentment.

"You know what the best part is?" Naomi said, sounding scarily earnest. "We can write the column Celeste Fanucci *wanted* to write. I mean, after I talked to her, I realized that kids need something like this. They need a forum to express themselves, not just to ask the usual advice-column questions, about boyfriends or whatever, but to ask about everything. About *issues*. About real life. You know? You'd be *great* at handling that."

I almost laughed. She was really pushing it now. But a thought was dawning on me: if Celeste had meant what she'd told Naomi—that she could use an advice columnist—and if Naomi became an advice columnist . . . well, odds were good that Celeste would write in to Naomi.

Which meant, of course, that she'd write to me.

And *that,* as Naomi had so archly observed the night before, was what I really wanted.

It was sort of perfect, in a twisted way. Yes. It was the alternative to stalking I'd been looking for. Celeste Fanucci would pour out her soul to me without knowing it. I would immerse myself in the intimate details of her life. More importantly, I would learn what she desired in a significant other. I would use this secret knowledge to transform myself before her eyes. I would *become* that significant other. And in the end I would bridge the unbridgeable chasm.

Sure, the chances of all that actually happening were approximately one in eight trillion. But I decided I might as well try. It wasn't like I had anything better to do. Neither did Naomi. I sighed, glancing around her rat hole of a room. Better to live for a dream than to wallow in reality, right? At the very least, as Naomi had pointed out, it could be fun.

"So what do you say?" she asked.

I shrugged. "If you think we can pull it off . . ."

She smiled wickedly. "We already have, Dave," she said. "Remember?"

Need help? Need advice?
Need to tell somebody that you're at the
END OF YOUR ROPE
and feel like SCREAMING?

TELL IT TO NAOMI!

Hey, we've all got problems. We've all got issues. Whether it's a fight with a best friend, a relationship gone sour, stress over college applications . . . life has a funny way of dishing out one crisis after another. Sometimes it gets to be a little too much. We at Roosevelt High know that. That's why we've decided to do something to help YOU.

Introducing Naomi . . . Roosevelt High's first advice columnist. Starting tomorrow, every Tuesday, right here on page 3, she will pick a question of yours and answer it. She will help you cope. Feel free to ask her ANYTHING. It doesn't just have to be about personal stuff, either. Whatever's on your mind—be it politics or religion, the environment or the economy—Naomi wants to hear from you. She wants to get you talking. She wants to get all of us talking. (Just as long as the conversation isn't dirty!) ☺

And who is Naomi? Well, she's a lot like you. She went to school right here at Roosevelt. She's lived in New York City all her life. If there's a problem out there, chances are she's dealt with it. And if she hasn't, she'll still figure out a way to relate. So if you've got drama, tell it to Naomi!

Write her at tellittonaomi@roosevelt.edu.

Chapter Eight

Somebody in our family was in a great mood.

I knew it as soon as I walked into our building Monday afternoon because I heard the frenzied cacophony of Jimi Hendrix's "Fire" coming down the stairwell. It was a little muffled, but even down in the lobby there was no mistaking the song—which meant it wasn't just being cranked; it was being *blasted*. By the time I reached our apartment, it sounded as if Jimi himself had risen from the grave to perform a live gig in apartment 4R.

Now, in normal families the blasting of "Fire" probably wouldn't mean a lot. But for us, Hendrix—particularly when played at a loud volume—takes on a deep, almost mystical significance. We all revere his music. Or rather, *each* of us reveres it. He is unique in this way. Mom and Aunt Ruth can tolerate the Strokes; I can tolerate Naomi's Michelle Branch collection (sort of); Naomi and I can both tolerate Sly and the Family Stone (on a limited rotation) . . . but Hendrix alone somehow does it for every family member—*individually*. I'm just as likely to carry around one of his CDs in my Discman as Mom and Aunt Ruth are.

The funny thing is, we've never acknowledged it. At least not out loud. The only time we ever talk about music at all is to rag on each other's lousy taste. But since we all *know* it, Hendrix's songs have become the unofficial soundtrack for any special occasion. Whenever we break fast at the end of Yom Kippur, whenever we rent a car to go upstate on vacation . . . pretty much whenever the four of us celebrate or have fun together as a family, Jimi is there, too. And there's never any discussion or debate. Somebody just puts on one of his CDs. It's gotten to the point where I could probably change the answer to the first of the four Passover questions: *Why is this night different from all other nights? Because on this night we hang out and bask in the glory of Jimi Hendrix's searing, psychedelic guitar.*

So when I first heard him down in the lobby, I knew something was up. Maybe Mom and Aunt Ruth had gotten raises. That was what had happened the last time I'd heard Hendrix down four flights of stairs ("The Wind Cries Mary," two years ago). Lord knows they were due for one. And now that I remembered, they'd also gotten off work early that day. . . .

I threw open the door.

The music was coming from Naomi's room.

Crap.

Mom and Aunt Ruth weren't even home.

There's nothing more irritating than when your older sister is happy for some reason, and you're not. That goes double when you're already annoyed with her. All you want to do is make an obscene gesture. Or at the very least, you want to know why she got her lame ex-boyfriend to run a moronic ad in the school paper without consulting you first, even though you're the one who's going to be writing the stupid advice column in the first place.

I trudged down the hall.

Naomi's door was cracked. She was hunched over her computer—in her pajamas, of course—whispering along to the lyrics. *"Let me stand next to your fire! Let me stand . . ."*

At least she'd opened her blinds. But the sun just spotlighted all the trash on the floor.

"Aren't you ever gonna clean this place?" I yelled.

Naomi jerked.

"Dude!" she yelled, laughing. She let out a deep sigh.

I scowled. "Please don't use that word."

"Why?" She scooted over to her stereo. "Cheese uses it all the time."

"Mm," I grunted.

Now I was even *more* annoyed. Naomi didn't know that Cheese and I were in a fight. I didn't want her to know. *I* didn't want to know. The weekend had come and gone, and I still hadn't heard from him. I knew he was home, too, because I saw his parents' SUV parked right in front of the building the whole time. He could have been sick, I supposed. Or he could have had a serious bug up his butt for no reason at all. One possibility was a lot more likely than the other.

"You're gonna give me high blood pressure if you sneak up on me like that," Naomi said once she'd turned the music down. "You scared me."

"You're scaring *me*. What are you so giddy about?"

Judging from her expression, you'd think I'd just asked the dumbest question in the world. "Didn't Joel tell you?" she asked.

"Tell me what? That he ran an ad in the school paper that makes me sound like a girly little wuss?"

"Oh, come on, Dave," she said. "There was nothing in the ad like that. Besides, you're pretending to be me, remember? So the ad doesn't make *you* sound like anything. And personally, I don't think it was girly at all." She glanced at the computer screen. "But, hey, don't take my word for it. Just check out the response."

My eyes narrowed. "What do you mean?"

She grinned.

I walked over to her monitor and peered at it.

```
You have 10 new messages.
Time: 3:32 pm  Subject: i owe my friend $573 dollars
Time: 3:33 pm  Subject: how do i transfer to different
     trig class
```

Time: 3:34 pm Subject: I LIVE IN A TOILET AND PAPA
    WEARS BANANA HAMMOCK BRIEFS
Time: 3:34 pm Subject: frightened of new york
Time: 3:35 pm Subject: (No Subject)
Time: 3:35 pm Subject: yo yo yo whaddup bee-atch!!!
Time: 3:36 pm Subject: my boyfriend smells
Time: 3:36 pm Subject: Fwd: fast food executives the
    REAL hate mongers
Time: 3:37 pm Subject: BOZ (Beard Of Zits)
Time: 3:37 pm Subject: i have this problem i play
    11 hours of Game Boy every day

I glanced at the clock in the lower right-hand corner of the screen. It was 3:38.

"Is this for real?" I asked.

Naomi started laughing. "These are just the ones I haven't opened yet. I've already gotten more than fifty. What did I tell you? You should read some of them. I didn't know kids your age were so . . . I don't know . . . all over the place."

I frowned. "Kids my age? Who are you, Aunt Ruth?"

"You know what I mean. It's a little scary."

My eyes flashed over the list again. I couldn't argue with her. Scary was putting it mildly. These looked disturbing. To be honest, I hadn't really expected anyone except Celeste to write in. Or maybe I'd just been hoping.

"Hey, wait a second," I said. "How come it doesn't say where the e-mails are from? I mean, how do you know who sent them?"

"I don't," Naomi said.

I turned to her. "What do you mean?"

"Joel set up the system to ensure anonymity. Well, actually, he got a friend who's a programmer to do it. But on the home page there's a little information bullet—"

"Whoa, whoa, slow down. The *system*? The *home page*?"

"Yeah," Naomi said.

"Uh, just out of curiosity, when were you guys planning on telling me about all this? And who said anything about anonymity?"

Naomi smiled and slouched back in the chair. "The system has to be anonymous, Dave. Otherwise nobody would write in. See, Joel and I did some research over the weekend. In order for an advice column to work—or any sort of therapy to work, really—the people who use it have to feel safe that their identities are kept secret. It's the only way they'll be honest. That's why so many kids wrote in. They know that 'Naomi' can't figure out who they are, so they can say whatever they want. But listen: this could turn into a gig for me. Joel has a friend at the *Village Voice,* an editor—and the guy said that the whole teen-column angle sounds like great story material. 'Very cutting edge,' he said. So he told Joel to tell me to send in some writing samples. . . ."

My jaw tightened. The more she rambled, the angrier I got. And it wasn't only because she and Joel Posterior-Massage had conducted their own "research" without me. She was just so slaphappy. She was acting like a little kid, like she'd gotten a puppy or something. I knew it had nothing to do with a potential gig at the *Village Voice,* either. She'd told me lots of times that those sorts of friend-of-a-friend connections were always tenuous at best. No, that wouldn't have made her glow like this. That wouldn't have prompted her to blast Hendrix—

"What?" she demanded, giggling. "Why are you giving me that look?"

"You're just acting sort of weird."

"*I'm* acting weird?" Naomi shook her head and stood. "Listen, Dave, I'm sorry we kept you out of the loop. It wasn't intentional. I just thought the technical side of things would bore you. I promise it won't happen again. But you know what? I think you should look through some of these. And maybe even answer one of them. I bet it'll make you feel better." She patted my back. She was trying to console me, but the way she placed her hand between my shoulders made me think of a ventriloquist with a dummy. "Maybe you'll find your friend Celeste in there."

I shook free. "How can I find Celeste?" I barked. "It's anonymous!"

"Okay, okay," she said softly. "I'm sorry. Why are you so grumpy?"

"I'm not grumpy," I muttered.

"Well, if it's because of all this, I apologize—really," she said. She headed for the door. "I'm going to get a snack. Hang out and go through the e-mails. Pick one and answer it, and we'll print it tomorrow. I'm telling you, I really think we could be on to something positive here. Your friends need help. . . ." Her voice trailed off as she shuffled down the hall.

My friends? I wondered, feeling disgustingly sorry for myself.

I slumped down in her chair.

Well, Naomi was certainly right about one thing. The kids at Roosevelt—friends or not—did need help. I almost prayed Celeste wasn't among them. They all sounded like candidates for institutionalization. I LIVE IN A TOILET AND PAPA WEARS BANANA HAMMOCK BRIEFS? *Good Lord.* Was there a PCP epidemic at school I didn't know about? I grabbed the mouse and clicked on the message.

Time: 3:34 pm

Subject: I LIVE IN A TOILET AND PAPA WEARS BANANA HAMMOCK BRIEFS

NAOMI!

PAPA SAY I SHOULD SEE YOUR DOCUMENT FIRST BUT IF YOU OFFER ADVICE I SHOULD LIKE TO RECIEVE IT. SORRY THAT IS RECEIVE. I BEFORE E EXCEPT AFTER C! I SHOULD LEAVE MISTAKE IN A CORRESPONDENCE TO SHOW THAT I TRY TO LEARN ENGLISH! CORRESPONDENCE IS A BIG TERM, NO? I

KNOW A FEW SLANGS SUCH AS <<WORD TO YOUR MOTHER.>> IT
IS DIFFICULT. I AM A STUDENT AT A SCHOOL THAT IS A
SCHOOL YOU ATTEND PAST THAT IS ROOSEVELT. I KNOW I
LEAVE OUT <<THE THE THE>> I FEAR THAT MAKES NOT
SENSE? I HAVE A PROBLEM I MENTION. OUR APARTMENT IS A
TOILET. PAPA WEARS NOT DRESS. HE WEARS ONLY THAT
WHICH I KNOW ARE TERMED BANANA HAMMOCK BRIEFS! HE IS
LICENSED TO ILL! HE DRINKS TOO MUCH VODKA NOW HE IS
SICK. HE GOES IN A HOSPITAL TODAY. MAMA IS IN PAU.
PAU IS A SMALL TOWN IN FRANCE WITH A GHETTO. I SHOULD
SAY PAU KEEPS IT REAL. IT IS DIFFICULT TO TELL. WE
ARE FROM ALGIERS WHO MOVE TO PAU TO TRAVAIL IN A
GARE. WE TALK ARABIC AND A SMALL GERMAN AND A SMALL
FRENCH. GARE IS RAILROAD STATION. I LOOK IT UP! PAPA
NOW HAS NOT A JOB IN A RAILROAD STATION NO MORE THAT
IS WHY PAPA AND I THEN MOVE TO UNITED STATES FOR A
JOB. HE HAS NOT A JOB IN UNITED STATES. HE IS SAD NOW.
HE GOES IN A HOSPITAL TODAY. I AM SCARED. I AM SAD.
HOW SHOULD I DO? MY NAME IS HOSPITAL GIRL. WORD TO
YOUR MOTHER.

SINCERELY YOURS
HOSPITAL GIRL

I tried to read it again, and then gave up about halfway through.
All the capital letters made me dizzy.

So, I thought miserably, *this is what it means to be an advice
columnist.*

I almost considered calling Joel Newbury and asking about the
school's policy regarding plagiarism, because this e-mail reminded me
a lot of a book Naomi had lent me over the summer by a fairly young
author who was being touted as the Next Big Novelist of Our Time.
One of the characters spoke and wrote in horribly broken English.
Reading that had made me dizzy. But it was definitely a lot more

enjoyable than reading *this*. There was just no way it could be true. (The parts I could understand, at least.) It was too tragic, too silly . . . too over-the-top.

As far as I could tell, Hospital Girl was trying to rip off this famous young author's style. And she wasn't doing a very good job. For one thing, her "slangs" had been outdated for about as long as Vanilla Ice's career had. (Vanilla Ice being the only person actually known to use the phrase "word to your mother.") The more I thought about it, the more I figured one of those cynical lit clubbers had written it as a gag—the Olga Romanoff crew, those chicks who think that they're the only people who read books, who drink coffee at the dump on Fourth Street and Avenue A and dress like they're sitting shivah for Goth rock. Maybe Olga herself had written it. Maybe she was trying to make an anti-advice-column "statement." *Whatever*. I clicked on the next message.

Time: 3:35 pm
Subject: frightened of new york

Dear Naomi,

I know everyone says this, but The Big Apple is making me paranoid. I'm convinced that a) every single bike messenger knows me personally and wants to run me over, b) the falafel guy on the corner charges me twice as much as he charges everyone else, and c) nobody at Roosevelt wants to be friends with me.

Yes, I'm new. But so are about 200 other kids. Every single freshman is new, right? What's wrong with me? It's not like I smell. I'm positive of this, because I just switched to a new brand of deodorant. I'm us-

ing stick instead of roll-on! There really is a difference. So what do I do? I'm shy. Do I move to Jersey?

—FONY (stands for Frightened of New York, and rhymes
with pony but hopefully doesn't mean "phony")

Much to my surprise, I found myself smiling.

At least *this* e-mail seemed genuine. It made me think of Celeste, too—the being new in school part of it, anyway. It couldn't be her, though; FONY was a freshman. And it definitely sounded too young for a senior. No . . . *young* is mean-spirited. *Young* is an adjective Olga Romanoff would probably use. It sounded funny and naive in that freshman sort of way. It sounded *honest*.

Unfortunately, it also made me realize that I'd never find Celeste by trolling for her e-mails. And that was pretty depressing, considering she was the only reason I'd agreed to this nonsense to begin with.

I leaned back in the chair.

I could hear Naomi puttering around in the kitchen.

I supposed that I *could* just answer FONY's letter. It would take about two minutes, tops.

I could also go to my room and wallow in loneliness. I'd been getting very good at that in the past few days. I'd hit a rhythm with it, an endless, monotonous rhythm, like those seventies *Shaft*-style funk songs Mom and Aunt Ruth loved so much . . . you know, a song with a title like "Dave Rosen Is Stuck in a Bad Funk"—with "Bad Funk" meaning two things (one positive, one negative), the way all those classic *Shaft*-style funk titles did.

Or I could call Cheese.

No. No freaking way. It was up to *him* to call *me*. True, this was the longest we'd ever gone without talking since we were six. (Even when we went on vacation, we still called or e-mailed each other, mostly to complain about the food outside New York.) But if Cheese thought that he could somehow punish me with the silent treatment just because I wouldn't hand over my guitar to some stupid kid I didn't even know . . . well . . . well, maybe it was best not to complete that thought.

Forget it. I clicked on the REPLY icon.

I was not going to obsess anymore about this Cheese BS. Nope. I had things to do. I had to counsel a perfect stranger who called herself FONY, for God's sake. I had a life, too.

```
Dear FONY,

A) Forget about Jersey. Come on, where would you
move? Atlantic City? It would be like living on a
giant Monopoly board. Also, Jersey is the official
birthplace of the mullet haircut. My apologies if you
have a mullet. (Then you really DO have problems.
Just kidding.☺)

B) As far as falafel goes, the guy on 20th and 5th is
your man. You'll know when you smell his cart. His
hot sauce will take you to Enlightenment and back.

C) Bike messengers want to mow down all pedestrians,
not just you. Well, unless you wronged one of them in
some way . . .

Okay, seriously. Don't laugh, but your fellow
Roosevelt students, new and old alike, are just as
shy as you are. They have an irrational fear of
strangers. Well, maybe it's not so much irrational as
natural. Or maybe it's both. People are always
frightened of something new—the way you're
frightened of New York. And I say the best way to
```

overcome any fear (natural OR irrational) is to
confront it. It's up to you to make the first move.

Remember Dr. Seuss? Remember the story about pale
green pants with nobody inside 'em? Just think of
somebody you want to meet as those pale green pants.
Walk up, right up, and introduce yourself. I mean,
what do you have to lose? They're pale green pants.
If they run away from you, it's their problem. At
least you're a human being, right?

Good luck and STAY AWAY FROM JERSEY,
Naomi

I didn't even bother to read it over. I'd second-guessed myself a
bunch of times when I'd written that sample, and in the end, there
was no point. The final version had ended up being pretty close to the
original. Best just to trust my instincts. I clicked on the SEND icon—

"Dave?"

I nearly fell off the chair.

Naomi stood right next to me, with a big grin on her face. She was
also holding a sheet of paper.

"Didn't you just tell me not to sneak up on you?" I mumbled.

"Man, you have deep concentration. You were in a zone. Can I
read what you wrote?"

"Why?"

"Don't worry," she said. "I'm not going to change a word. That's
why I waited until you were finished. But I almost forgot—you have
to sign this. Joel faxed it to me this morning."

I scowled. "I have to sign something? Why? Am I going to be tes-
tifying in court?"

"It's nothing," Naomi said, flapping the form in front of me. "It's
called a nondisclosure agreement. Joel just wants to make sure you

don't tell anyone that I'm the same Naomi as the Naomi in the column."

"But you aren't," I said.

"I know. But Joel doesn't know that. He's worried, since he thinks you and I tried to pull off a scam earlier. It's not that he doesn't trust you . . . it's just, you know, since he thinks that you pretended to be me the other day, he thinks maybe now you might tell someone that you're *related* to Naomi."

I shook my head, completely baffled. "Who would I tell?"

"Just sign the stupid agreement," she groaned. "What's your problem?"

"My problem? Gee, Tell-It-to-Naomi, I don't know. Maybe my problem is that I'm at the *end of my rope* and I feel like *screaming*. Can you help me out?"

She laughed. "Look, Dave, it's just . . . see, I'm having dinner with Joel later tonight, and it would make things easier if you signed this now. That way you won't have to give it to him tomorrow at school. That's why he faxed it here. He doesn't want to deal with it *there*. He doesn't want there to be any possible connection between you and me and him, so—"

"Wait, wait," I interrupted. "You're going on a date with Joel Newbury?"

She blinked. Her hand fell to her side. "It's not a date," she said. "It's dinner."

A foul realization was dawning on me. "My God. Is that why you were cranking Hendrix? Is that why you want to tell the world you're so happy?"

Naomi blushed. This was not a good sign. I hadn't seen my sister's face turn red in over six years—not since the afternoon we'd walked in on Aunt Ruth making out with the plumber.

"I have no idea what you're talking about," she said after a moment. "I just felt like listening to that new greatest hits collection. Speaking of which, I had to go get it from your room. You borrowed it without asking. You always borrow my crap without asking."

It was an old tactic of hers: shift the attention to me when things go wrong. But for once, her talent for lying had failed. *Ugh.* It was painfully clear. Not only was she going on a date with Joel Newbury, *she* still had the hots for *him*. And that . . . well, that defied logic. Couldn't she see what a little wiener he was? This was the same guy who'd radically altered his appearance just because she'd jokingly compared him to Jerry Seinfeld. And that was the least of his offenses. That was actually positive. What about this ridiculous form I had to sign? Forget wiener; he was a psycho.

"Look, are you gonna sign this or not?" Naomi demanded. She couldn't stop smiling.

"I'll sign it," I mumbled.

And I have to admit: I couldn't help smiling back at her. At least somebody around here *really* had a life. Regardless of the reason, that was a good thing. The rest of us were just faking.

Chapter Nine

Tuesday gave me the first clue as to the madness that would follow. Not that I had any idea *then*. No, on that one, brief, happy day— the day the school paper ran its very first installment of "Tell It to Naomi!"—the whole insane scheme seemed pretty harmless. And fun. And sort of flattering, too, if you want to know the truth.

There wasn't much to the column, just the e-mail FONY had sent me, and then my response. Joel had taken care of all the downloading and formatting—the "technical side," in Naomi's words. In the end, it didn't look all that different from the ad that had appeared the day before: same font, same general layout . . . same everything.

I didn't really expect anyone to pay any attention to it. I definitely didn't expect anyone to talk about it. But after lunch I began to hear little snippets of conversation in the halls:

"The hot sauce on Twentieth and Fifth once made me hallucinate. . . ."

". . . gonna go up to that honey in biology and be like, 'Yo, I got on my pale green pants. Wanna know what's inside 'em?"

"*Everybody* is too shy around here, and I'm glad somebody finally said it. . . ."

I overheard my sister's name a lot, too. "Naomi" seemed to be on everyone's lips, wafting through the air like a juicy bit of gossip. I even caught Olga Romanoff—outside the classroom where the lit club meets, no less—asking her coffee-shop minions: "Hello? Is there anything more heinous than a mullet? Or Jersey in general? I mean, come on. You guys have read Philip Roth."

It was nuts. There was a real, palpable *buzz*.

And I was responsible for it. *Me*. Mr. Invisibility. The guy who'd made it through freshman year without getting to know a single person beyond "Hey, what's up?" I found myself chuckling out loud a few times. There's just something so undeniably cool about knowing a secret that no one else could possibly ever guess. It was like being Clark Kent.

But there was a downside to that. Clark Kent could never admit to being Superman. And let's face it: he was a geek. He was cut off from people. He never quite fit in. Likewise, I wasn't exactly the star of Roosevelt. Everybody was talking about the column except me. And it wasn't because I'd signed that moronic nondisclosure agreement. It was for the simple reason that I had nobody to talk *to*.

I wondered how FONY felt.

I wondered who she *was,* more than anything. I kept eyeing insecure-looking freshman girls. (In retrospect, probably not the wisest idea.) I imagined that someday—two years from now, when I was a senior and FONY was a junior—both of us would be cool and popular and comfortable. We would be tight friends. (Oh, and I would also be going out with Celeste, who would have forsaken college just to stay with me.) But we wouldn't know the truth. And then in a rare confessional moment, we would break down and spill. And we would hug each other.

The frightening thing was, this lunatic daydream made me feel *better*.

I even exchanged a conspiratorial grin with Joel as we passed each other on the stairs before final period. He'd taken my sister to one of those skanky Indian restaurants on Sixth Street, where they blast off-kilter disco and the odds of contracting a fatal gastrointestinal disease are about fifty-fifty. (According to Naomi, they'd had a "great time.")

If I could bring myself to smile at Joel Newbury after *that*—tossing in the high probability that he'd managed at least one cheap ass-grab during the evening—well, I must have been in a good mood.

It wouldn't last long.

* * *

Celeste Fanucci was sick that Tuesday. Or *something*. She definitely wasn't in school, because I didn't see her once.

I saw her the next day, though.

Boy, did I see her.

In order to fully illustrate the abomination of what happened, I have to set the stage a little:

Last year in freshman English, we were assigned to read *1984,* by George Orwell. I guess it's one of those classics that everybody has to read sooner or later. In a nutshell, it's about a repressive society where everybody has to think and act the same way, and they're all suspicious of each other, and they're constantly being spied on and encouraged to do evil by the vicious powers that be. (Sort of like one of those reality *Spring Break!* specials, minus the glamour and midriff shots.)

In the story there's a place called Room 101. It's where you get sent for the ultimate torture. The scary part is that you don't know what the torture will be—not exactly. You only know it'll be "the worst thing in the world." It's different for everybody. It depends upon what you're afraid of most. They tailor-make the torture to fit you personally.

So after reading about Room 101, I wondered what "the worst thing in the world" would be for me. For the main character in the book it was rats, which I didn't quite get. Sure, rats are gross, but in New York City they're about as common as tourists—and in certain cases, preferable. But for me . . . what? Lima beans? "Smooth jazz"? Being forced to wear Grandpa Meyer's toupee?

I never imagined I'd actually find out.

But that's exactly what happened on Wednesday. The school cafeteria became my Room 101—and true to *1984,* "the worst thing in the world" turned out to be something so horrifying and inconceivable that I would never have even *dreamed* of it.

It was the sight of Celeste Fanucci sitting alone at a table with Zeke Beck.

Only they weren't just sitting together.

She was holding his hand.

Compared to seeing that, wearing Grandpa Meyer's toupee would have been a freaking joy.

Zeke Beck was Jed Beck's older brother. He was pretty much just a bigger and swarthier version of Jed—the main difference being a dopey hippie vibe he'd honed with fuzzy sweaters and a fuzzy beard. (To his credit, the beard was *thick*. Old-time rabbi thick.) He was also a self-proclaimed singer/songwriter: always key for a hippie. And like Jed, he was supposed to be a notorious ladies' man. Not that I knew this for sure. I did once overhear a girl screaming at him in the hall, calling him an ass-face because he'd made out with her sister. Or maybe it was her cousin. Whatever. As a senior, he was so far removed from my own realm of existence that I'd never given him much thought. Jed was in my grade, and we'd taken chemistry together, so I'd dealt firsthand with his particular brand of schmuck-ness . . . like, say for instance, the time he told me I didn't "talk like other guys." But Zeke and I had never taken a class together. And we never would. He might as well have gone to a different school.

I wished he'd gone to a different school, the jerk.

I stood there in the middle of the cafeteria, clutching my lunch tray. Hope circled the proverbial drain like dirty bathwater. Celeste was holding Zeke's hand with both of hers. She was *gazing* at it. She was *stroking* it.

Then they both laughed.

At that moment I seriously considered dropping out of Roosevelt. Why not? If school was a "job," as Cheese and I had decreed in our pact, I had the right to quit. People quit their jobs all the time. It was *cool* to quit a job you didn't like. It gave you a kind of maverick nobility, the chance to become a real, honest-to-goodness rebel.

Celeste turned to me. Her eyes met mine.

She dropped Zeke's hand and beckoned me toward her table.

At first I thought she was waving at someone else.

I glanced over my shoulder. "Me?" I mouthed.

She nodded, laughing.

I swallowed and did my best to ignore Zeke Beck's puzzled frown. By the time I made it to the rear of the cafeteria, my knees were wobbling.

"Hey, Dave," Celeste said brightly.

"Hi," I said. At least she got my name right this time.

She glanced at Zeke. "Hey, do you guys know each other? Dave, this is Ezekiel."

Ezekiel? I forced a pained smile. "Hey," I said.

"What's up, bro?" Zeke bellowed. He returned the smile, clearly only for Celeste's sake.

"So, listen, Dave, I have to ask you something," Celeste said. She spoke in a stage whisper. "The Naomi who wrote the column yesterday . . . that's your sister, right?"

I avoided her eyes. "Uh—I don't know what you're talking about."

Celeste laughed. "Come on. You can tell me. I swear it won't leave this table."

"The—uh, column?" I asked

"Yeah, bro, the column," Zeke said. "You've seen it, right?"

"Uh—I don't think so. No."

"You *haven't?*" they both asked at the same time.

"Jinx!" Zeke shouted.

Celeste giggled.

I shrugged. "No," I repeated weakly. "I haven't seen it." *Real convincing, there, Dave,* I thought. I probably sounded a lot like Cain did when he was asked if he'd seen Abel around anywhere. *Note to self: work on lying.*

"Well, you must be the only one left," Zeke said. "You should check it out." He shifted his gaze to Celeste. "It made me realize that

I was a jackass for being so shy. It made me walk right up to these pale green pants and introduce myself."

Celeste giggled again.

I wanted to barf.

Horrifyingly enough, she *was* wearing pale green pants. Corduroys. I had a vivid fantasy of smashing my tray full of meat loaf and mashed potatoes over Zeke's, aka Ezekiel's, head.

"Aw, come on, Dave," Celeste said. "I swear we won't tell, okay?" Her voice was oddly intimate—almost too much so—but in a familial way. You'd think *she* was my older sister. It was a nightmare. "I know this must be weird for you. I mean, I already talked to Mr. Newbury, so I know the whole deal. He doesn't want anybody to know who Naomi really is. He won't even admit that Naomi is her real name!" She laughed and brushed her curls out of her eyes. "But I spoke to your sister on the phone, remember? So I know that she and Mr. Newbury are friends. So . . . ?"

Before I could think of another lame excuse, Zeke took Celeste's hand. He stretched it out in his own, slowly and deliberately—as if he were conducting a palm reading. Then he leaned across the table. He brought his fuzzy face within about six inches of Celeste's nose. He made a big point of ignoring me.

I almost laughed. *Nice work, Ezekiel! Very smooth! Subtle, too!* If he wanted me to take a hike, he could just tell me. Not that I needed any encouragement. Nope. I was on my way. Maybe there was some mathematical correlation between facial hair and brainpower: the more you had of one, the less you had of the other.

"It doesn't really matter who Naomi is," Zeke said to Celeste in a breathy voice. (If he was trying to be sexy, it wasn't working. He sounded like a serial killer in one of those *American Justice* reenactments.) "All's I know is she's a genius. I haven't thought of Dr. Seuss in so long. The thing about him . . . he's a true artist. He's a surrealist. He's up there with Dalí. He taps into reality in a totally skewed way, and that makes his art more real. Reading him and looking at those pictures is like . . . I don't know—interpreting a dream or something."

Dalí? Interpreting a dream?

And his little brother said *I* didn't talk like other guys?

Ten to one Zeke had looked up surrealism on the Internet right before lunch and was now regurgitating some tripe he'd gotten off an SAT study site. Listening to him made *me* want to regurgitate. No, actually—what made me want to regurgitate was the way Celeste gazed dreamily back at him, as if he somehow made sense.

"Hey, Ezekiel, why don't you read Dave's palm?" Celeste suddenly asked.

My eyes narrowed.

Zeke blinked at her.

"Ezekiel just taught me how to read palms," Celeste stated with complete sincerity. She pulled her hand from his and turned to me. "You want to talk surreal? I couldn't believe how accurate it was. You should try it. You'll freak out."

I already am *freaking out,* I thought.

Wow. This was no longer just a nightmare. This was hell: one of those rare times in life where you make an absurd joke and forget it— and the very next instant you discover that it's true. *This* was surreal.

Zeke Beck really *was* giving Celeste a palm reading.

And vice versa.

That's what they were actually *doing.*

The guy was smooth. No doubt about it. The palm-reading angle? I *never* would have thought of that. No, instead, I'd come up with a bugged-out ruse involving various lies, my sister, an ass-grabber, and a phony advice column. That was my brilliant strategy to woo Celeste Fanucci. Man, I could learn a thing or two from Zeke Beck. He wasn't as dumb as I thought. Not by a long shot. No wonder he'd decided to start calling himself by his full name. He could tell people's fortunes now. He'd become a full-on *prophet.*

"I'd love for Ezekiel to read my palm," I said. "But I'm seeing my astrologer this afternoon, and he always gets pissed off when I ask for a second opinion."

Celeste glanced at Zeke.

For a terrible instant I was worried I'd offended her. (I knew where I stood with him.) But then she burst out laughing. She slipped into old-drunk mode again, slamming her fist on the table. Her bracelets jangled. A tear fell from her cheek.

Zeke just smiled. His eyes were like two blocks of ice.

I took the opportunity to turn and bolt, brave soul that I was. My plate nearly slid off my tray.

"I'll see you guys later!" I yelled over my shoulder.

Celeste kept cackling away.

"Yeah, later, bro," Zeke called after me.

I'm pretty sure he meant we should see each other *much* later—if at all. Either that or he meant to kick my ass. Realistically I'd have to say the latter. So on the plus side, I didn't need one of his palm readings to glimpse the future. No, it was all taking shape before me, as clear as a crystal ball: Ezekiel Beck—prophet, singer/songwriter, surrealist, Seuss lover . . . the New Age guru with the washboard abs—was going to pulverize me. And somewhere down the line he would start dating the one girl at school I actually cared about.

But hey, at least the future couldn't get any worse, right?

Ha, ha.

I should have known not to ask myself stupid questions like that.

Chapter Ten

All during last period the sky began to darken. The clouds came together in that certain evil grayish black swirl—like the cafeteria's mashed potatoes—when you know it's not just going to rain, it's going to *pour*. Sure enough, five minutes before the final bell the floodgates opened. I hadn't brought a raincoat, of course. So I did what I always did in those circumstances: I loitered on the steps with all the other unprepared chumps, praying for a miracle—and then I gave up and ran the ten blocks home, splashing and cursing.

That's when I saw Cheese for the first time since our fight.

It had been one full week.

He was scurrying downstairs to the lobby. Some kid was with him. I wondered if it was that "sick" guitarist. Not that it mattered. No, whoever it was, I got the picture: our pact about school was now officially kaput. Cheese was no longer simply befriending his coworkers; he was taking his job home with him.

I wiped my dripping nose with a wet sleeve. Neither Cheese nor his friend was wearing a raincoat. They weren't carrying umbrellas, either. Odder still, they looked like they were playing dress-up. Both had on identical black suit jackets, thick black belts, Doc Martens. . . . Even their brown bangs were the same length. Maybe this kid was an only child, too. Maybe he and Cheese were trying to make up for their lack of siblings by pretending to be twins.

"Hey," I said.

"What's the dilly, son?" Cheese asked.

I couldn't tell if he was talking to me or the other guy. He'd never called me "son" before—but I suppose it was an improvement over "dude." And "dilly"? . . . I decided to start from scratch.

"What's up?" I said.

"Crime," the other guy answered.

Both he and Cheese laughed. I watched as they strolled right past me.

"You know, it's pouring outside," I said.

Cheese shrugged. "It's *real,* son."

The other guy pushed through the door and marched out into the rain. Cheese trailed behind him. I felt the same nausea I'd felt when Naomi had suggested there were a hundred wiseasses just like Cheese at Roosevelt. Maybe she was right. Maybe there were. Clearly, I had no idea what kind of a wiseass he was anymore. I supposed I should be happy for him, though: new friends, new look, new language—a language that wasn't even linguistically related to MTV Award Show Speak. I'd barely understood a word he'd said.

Later, son! I yelled silently.

At the last moment Cheese hesitated in the doorway. He turned to me. I couldn't see his eyes. His hair hung practically to his nose.

"Yeah?" I said, giving him one more chance.

He shook his head. "Nothing," he mumbled.

"Where are you going, anyway?" I asked.

"I'm going to look for a place that sells waterproof microphones," he said. "I want to stage-dive into a big vat of gravy. You know, when the time comes to perform live. But I can only pay by homemade personal check. Or the barter system."

In spite of the heinousness of it all, I laughed. I hated myself for it.

"Come on, Greg," the other guy called.

My jaw dropped. *"Greg?"* I cried. "Whoa . . . wait. *Greg?"*

Cheese chewed his lip. "It's my name, Dave," he said.

I had no idea how to respond to that.

As it turned out, I didn't have to. Cheese looked up at me as if to add something—then turned and slunk out the door, disappearing with his twin into the storm.

* * *

Upstairs, I found Naomi frantically pacing the front hall and muttering to herself. She'd probably lost her wallet. She'd been doing that a lot lately. It looked as if *she* were playing dress-up, too. She had on a formal, professional-type black pantsuit, and her hair was actually brushed. And she was wearing eyeliner. She hardly ever wore makeup. She hadn't even worn any for her date with Joel Newbury.

"Have you seen my wallet?" she asked.

"I'd say check your room, but I wouldn't go in there without a survival kit. What's going on?"

"I'm supposed to meet Joel's friend from the *Village Voice* right now," she grumbled. She started rooting through the basket full of keys we keep by the door. "I'm seriously late."

"You can borrow a couple of bucks from me if you want," I offered.

"Really?" She flashed me an eager smile. "Are you sure?"

"Yeah, it's no big deal."

She sighed. "Thanks, Dave."

I shrugged and dug through my pocket, pulling out a few crumpled bills. It wasn't a big deal at all, in fact. Nope. It wasn't like I needed the cash this afternoon. I sure as hell didn't have anyone to meet, or rain to get caught in, or bands to start with clones.

"You're a lifesaver," Naomi said. She grabbed the money from me and strode toward the door, her heels clattering. "Hey, is it still raining?"

"It's real, son."

She glanced over her shoulder. "Huh?"

"Yeah, it's still raining," I said as I dripped.

Her nose wrinkled. "Are you okay?" she asked.

"Never better."

"Really?" She reached into the closet for an umbrella. "You seem sort of bummed."

"Life is peachy," I said.

"You *are* bummed. And who says *peachy*? Oh, I almost forgot! I have some news that will cheer you up. Joel just called. He told me that the response to the first column blew his mind. He said maybe two dozen kids have come up to him in the past two days asking who Naomi is." She laughed. "He said that the column single-handedly got the student body to start reading the school paper again. They ran out of copies of yesterday's edition! Isn't that awesome?"

Awesome?

I could think of another word. Call me sour, but I couldn't find it "awesome" that so many kids were so psyched about something *I'd* done and Joel Newbury was somehow taking credit for. Or at least partial credit.

"Dave?" Naomi prompted.

I faked a big smile. "Yeah!" I exclaimed. "Awesome!"

She smirked. "You have to get over this problem you have with Joel," she said. "He's not a bad guy. You just have to get to know him. Give him a chance."

"I didn't say anything," I protested.

"Yeah, you did," she said gently. She glanced at her watch. "Damn. All right, I gotta go. But look, Joel told me that he wants the column to run daily instead of weekly. He's really excited. He says he can use it to transform the whole school paper. I told him I had to think about it. But you know . . . it could be really cool. I mean, I never imagined this whole thing would take off so fast. So let's you and me talk later. I'll be back in, like, two hours. My computer is on if you want to go through the e-mails we got today. And thanks again for the money. Cheer up, all right?"

She slammed the door behind her.

I blinked.

A small puddle of rainwater had begun to form at my feet.

Well.

At a time like this—after school on a typical Wednesday, the "hump" day, if you will—a young man sometimes takes stock of how his week is going thus far. He might think of ways to improve it.

I could think of several. I could order fifty pounds of lima beans and wolf them all down until my stomach exploded in a slimy green bloodbath. That would be an improvement. I could impale myself on a ground-up collection of smooth jazz CDs. Yes, that was another option. Then there were rats. . . . *Hmm.* For some reason I couldn't seem to come up with any improvements that didn't involve my own gruesome death.

But, hey, what did I have to be so depressed about? Joel wanted to run the column daily! Great! I could entertain Celeste and Zeke five times a week instead of just once! And if all it took was that first short response to FONY to bring the two lovebirds together—to help Zeke overcome his shyness and to compel Celeste to wear those pale green pants . . . well, gee! Think of how fast their torrid romance would blossom if they could soak up my "genius" (yes, Prophet Beck's actual word, if you remember) *every single day of the goddamn year*!

I had nothing to be depressed about.

Nope. Life wasn't just peachy. Life was wonderful. Life was *sublime.*

Once again, I could see the future without the aid of a palm reading: Naomi would soon return home from her triumphant meeting at the *Village Voice,* having landed the perfect gig there, something in the six-figure range. Plus, she'd have already secured a film deal and book contract about her so-called cutting-edge teen advice column—which meant, of course, that "Tell It to Naomi!" would definitely have to run daily. Which also meant my own work was cut out for me. I'd have to answer roughly 43,281 e-mails a day with subject headings like "yo yo yo whaddup bee-atch!!!" On the plus side, our family would move to that fabulous new apartment in a doorman/elevator building we'd been fantasizing about. On the minus side, Joel Newbury would move in with us, since he and Naomi would have eloped—

My ears perked up.

There was faint laughter outside in the stairwell, gravelly and all too familiar . . . But, no, it couldn't be. Not this early in the day.

"Who wears heels in the pouring rain?" a voice asked.

It *was*.

The lock clicked. The door flew open.

Mom and Aunt Ruth shambled into the apartment: a dripping, unwieldy mass of matching yellow rain gear.

"Dave!" Aunt Ruth cried. "Guess what? We got a raise!"

My eyes widened. I wasn't sure why, but I felt as if I'd been socked in the stomach.

Mom swept me into her arms and kissed me on the cheek. "Isn't it wonderful? We weren't even expecting—" She broke off and pulled away from me. "Dave, you're soaking. Didn't you listen to the weather report this morning?"

"I . . . I guess—"

"Mr. Schwartz buzzed us in right after lunch," Aunt Ruth interrupted, out of breath. "At first your mother and I thought we were going to be fired! But he was all smiles, so we just knew the news was good. He asked about you, too, Dave." She squirmed out of her coat and boots and left them in a heap by the door. "You remember Mr. Schwartz, don't you? Our boss? The fellow with the mole on his chin?"

"You're going to catch pneumonia," Mom scolded me. She tossed her wet raincoat on top of Aunt Ruth's. "You should dry yourself off, no?"

I shrugged. "I'm okay."

"I vote we all go out to dinner tonight to celebrate," Aunt Ruth said. She padded into the kitchen in her stocking feet. "Where do you want to go, Dave? That Chinese place on Second Avenue? Or Don Vito's? Anywhere you want. The sky's the limit. Where's Naomi running off to, by the way? We just passed her outside. The hurry she's in! We didn't even have a chance to tell her."

"She, uh . . . she's going to meet a friend of that guy who teaches at my school. . . ."

"Guess how much Mr. Schwartz gave us," Mom whispered. As if by magic, she produced a towel. She handed it to me, smiling joyously. "A fifteen percent pay increase! Both of us!"

"That's . . . um, fantastic."

"Where did you say Naomi was going?" Aunt Ruth called.

I opened my mouth, but the staccato opening riff of "Purple Haze" suddenly blared from the kitchen stereo: *baow!-BAOW!-baow!-BAOW!-baow!-BAOW!* . . . (If you're not a Jimi Hendrix fan—and at that moment I wasn't sure if *I* was—take it from me: that opening is by far the weirdest, most dissonant guitar line he ever recorded. Even at a reasonable volume it makes you feel like you're being trampled by a circus parade. So there wasn't much point in trying to answer her.)

"Dry off and come celebrate with us, okay?" Mom yelled over the music. She gave me another quick peck on the cheek and hurried to join Aunt Ruth.

I wanted to go celebrate with them. I honestly did. This was good news. *Great* news. But if I went in there, I'd just spoil the party. And they deserved to party.

We all deserved to party.

No—on second thought, that wasn't quite true. Mom and Aunt Ruth deserved to party because they'd *earned* something. They'd worked their butts off, and they'd successfully accomplished their mission: to bring home more money so that all of our lives would be better.

Mazel tov to them.

And if Naomi landed a gig at the *Village Voice,* then she deserved to party, too.

Mazel tov to her.

Even Cheese deserved to party. He'd accomplished *his* mission. He'd met the right new people to start an actual, nonjoke band. (True, the mission forsook everything he'd once stood for, and those right new people were idiots, but I had to give him credit.)

I was the only one who didn't deserve to party.

I hadn't accomplished any mission. I didn't even *have* a mission—which was the problem. Sure, moping around and fantasizing about humorous forms of suicide occupied my time . . . but in the end it got me as far as practicing guitar. I needed a concrete, realistic *goal*. I needed a reason to get up every morning, to smile at myself in the mirror after I brushed my teeth and say, "You're one step closer." I needed—

That's when it hit me.

Yes.

It was the same kind of epiphany I'd had a week earlier, when I'd come up with the whole advice column idea in the first place. And it was as clear to me as the lines on Celeste Fanucci's palm must have been to Zeke Beck.

It would solve all my problems. It would take my mind off Cheese (sorry—"Greg") and his new clones. It would clue me in to insights I could never have even *imagined*. But most importantly, it would allow me to focus on what truly mattered: namely Celeste herself.

I'd wanted to write an advice column, right? I'd gotten *myself* into this mess, hadn't I?

So I would make the most of it.

I would harness the column's power. People wouldn't tell it to Naomi. I would tell it to *them*. I would use the column—subtly, delicately, but also very obviously—to show everyone at Roosevelt High what a fool Zeke Beck was. But I wouldn't mention his name, of course. Oh, no. I would be very very clever. Because if all it took was Dr. Seuss to get two strangers talking, to get this ridiculous buzz started around the halls . . . well, imagine what I could do if I actually put some careful thought into my responses?

Yes. It *was* awesome that Joel wanted to run the column daily. It was a blessing. Because FONY, Hospital Girl—all of them would be transformed. They would become the tools I would wield to dig an unbridgeable chasm—a *truly* unbridgeable chasm—between Zeke and Celeste. Whatever a kid's problem or question, my advice would always include the same subliminal message: palm-reading morons were not right for beautiful brand-new seniors. No. Witty, sensitive, Hendrix-loving sophomores who didn't talk like other guys were. And everyone who read the column (yes, you, Celeste!) would soon come to see this as the Truth.

And they wouldn't even know it.

It was brilliant.

Or like all good epiphanies, it was completely twisted.

Or it was both. But I had my mission.

"Am I happy or in misery?" Jimi sang from the kitchen. *"Whatever it is, that girl put a spell on me. . . ."*

***

```
You have 71 new messages
Time: 7:12 pm
Subject: cow-sized thighs, no life
Time: 7:12 pm
Subject: i smell my stanky gym shorts and its mm-mm good
Time: 7:13 pm
Subject: mom = my new "best friend" = my worst nightmare
Time: 7:13 pm
Subject: another paranoid rambling note from FONY
Time: 7:13 pm
Subject: my shorty thinks her hooters are too damn
         small yo!!!
Time: 7:13 pm
Subject: don't tell this to anyone or I will kill you
Time: 7:13 pm
Subject: underage/open container violation/ wine
         coolers/need lawyer . . .
Time: 7:14 pm
Subject: PAPA SAY YOU ARE EVIL
Time: 7:14 pm
Subject: friends? what friends?
Time: 7:14 pm
Subject: FWD: if you want to see two nympho college
         girls taking a bath

(to view messages 11-20, click here)
```

Chapter Eleven

My mission ended up being a little more complicated than I'd expected.

The first inkling of a possible snag came the following night. We'd just returned from our big celebratory feast at Don Vito's. Mom and Aunt Ruth had decided to postpone the Mr.-Schwartz's-raise blowout from Wednesday to Thursday because the rain wouldn't stop. Also, Naomi didn't get back from her meeting at the *Village Voice* until nine.

Coincidentally, Joel's friend turned out to be a guy Naomi had known from journalism school . . . Brian Something. We'd never heard of him. He didn't offer her a gig, either. She didn't even know it was going to be the same Brian until she saw him face to face. But she did say that they "got into an amazing conversation about recycling on the Upper West Side"—which was why she came home so late.

I had a feeling she wasn't telling us the whole story. Even factoring in the Mafia, it's tough to imagine *any* conversation about recycling being amazing, much less taking up five whole hours. I wondered if she and Brian had hit it off in more than just a nostalgic, it's-funny-we-bumped-into-each-other kind of way. I hoped so. Brian Something might have been friends with Joel Newbury, but he *wasn't* Joel Newbury. And as far as I was concerned, that made him an ideal match for my sister.

But back to Thursday:

The moment we arrived home, Naomi whisked me straight to her room. Or maybe not "whisked." Both of us had eaten too much pasta for any whisking. "Dragged" is more like it. Naomi collapsed onto her unmade bed with a grunt. I brushed the day's garbage off the desk and slumped down at her computer.

"I don't know why I always do it," she said.

"Do what?"

"Let Mom and Aunt Ruth take us to Don Vito's. I always swear I'm only gonna eat half the eggplant parm and take the rest home. And I always end up scarfing down the whole plate. The portions are too big. Who eats that much?"

"*You* do," I said, rubbing my aching belly. "But it's not your fault. You know how the walls are lined with all those photos of big fat guys with big fat smiles? See, the people at Don Vito's are geniuses. It's like hypnosis. You sit there waiting for the food to arrive. In the meantime, you look all around and you say to yourself, 'Wow, these guys on the wall look so happy. I bet I know the reason. They don't just live life. They *eat* life—in huge, heaping portions. And I want to be just like them—'"

"Shut up," Naomi groaned. "Don't make me laugh. It hurts too much."

I clicked on to the Internet.

That's when I saw it.

"Tell It to Naomi!" had seventy-one new messages.

Which meant they had all arrived since we'd last checked—right before we'd gone to dinner. *Only two hours ago.*

"Oh, my God," I said.

"What?"

"I . . . I don't . . ." I shook my head. "You know, maybe this isn't such a great idea. Running the column daily, I mean. It's just—it's going to be a lot of work."

"Why, what happened?" Naomi asked. She forced herself to sit up.

I scooted aside so she could see the screen. "Check it out."

She started smiling.

"I don't have time for this," I muttered. "I have homework."

"Hey, man, I'm telling you, you have a gift for offering advice—"

"Don't," I interrupted. "I ate too much. I already feel sick."

"Dave, come on," she said. "You don't have to answer all those e-mails. You don't even have to read them. Just skim through the list, and pick—I don't know—like, three that look interesting. Use your favorite one for the column, and reply to the other two just to be polite. You know, so your audience thinks you care." She laughed. "You're famous, man. You gotta learn to deal with it."

I turned and frowned at her.

"What?" she said.

"You're using that tone of voice again."

"What tone of voice?"

"The infomercial tone. Like you're trying to con me into buying some schlock. I mean, I'm not famous. . . ." I turned back to the screen. For an instant I experienced an impossible mix of delight and misery. "And even if I *were* famous, I wouldn't want to trick my audience into thinking that I care about their problems when all I'm really doing is pretending—"

"I didn't say that!" Naomi yelled.

"So what did you say?"

Naomi chuckled. She flopped back down on the bed. "Nothing. It's just that you don't have to stress about any of this. You're not the kind of person who *would* trick people, even if you tried. But look. If you want, I'll pick out the e-mails for you. Even better, I'll go through the inbox every night and pick out three: one for the column, two to be polite. I'll set it all up for you. Okay? How's that sound?"

It sounds terrible, I thought, suddenly ashamed.

The Italian food churned in my stomach. Naomi was wrong: I already had tricked people, without trying at all. More to the point, I had to *keep* tricking them. My mission depended on it. I couldn't let Naomi pick out the e-mails for me, because she wouldn't know to look for the ones that could best be used to send my subliminal anti–Zeke Beck message to Celeste. And if Naomi ever found out

what my true intentions were, if *anybody* ever found out . . . *Jeez.* No, that could never happen. So I had to go through all the e-mails personally. Besides, at the very least I had to *try* to care about the kids who wrote in—if not for Naomi's sake, then for myself. Otherwise I would descend into a world of slime I'd imagined was inhabited only by the likes of . . . well, say, Zeke Beck.

"It's really not that big a deal," Naomi said. "I don't mind. It's actually better this way. Joel told me he's been talking to a therapist at one of those teen hotlines. He's setting it up so he and I can refer the kids with the serious problems to somebody who can deal with them."

I wasn't following. I was barely listening. "Huh?"

Naomi giggled. "Suffering from a little food coma, are we? I *said,* I wouldn't mind going through the e-mails and picking out some for you. And then I can show them to Joel. It might be a good thing if he got involved. . . ." Her voice trailed off. She sighed. "He really loves this column. You know that? He really feels like he's doing something important at school, which is great for a new teacher."

Something in her sigh made my churning stomach clench with sudden, violent pain. I swiveled around in the chair.

"So what did you and Brian What's-His-Face *really* talk about?" I asked.

She blinked. "What?"

"I mean, why did you really hang out with him for five hours?" I smiled. "And don't tell me it was to talk about recycling on the Upper West Side. I can tell when you're lying. Did he ask you out?"

Naomi's face shriveled up. She looked like she'd just caught a whiff of one those landfills on the New Jersey Turnpike. "*What?* Where did you get *that* idea?"

My smile disappeared. "I . . . I just—"

"It was an *interview*," she said. "Besides, he's not my type." She cringed. "Not even close. I mean, he's a really cool guy—a *really* cool guy—but, he, ah . . . whatever."

"Oh, come on," I pressed, refusing to give up. "You talked to him for five hours."

She didn't say a word.

Slowly her cheeks turned pink, then red. Soon they were glowing like two stoplights—just like when we'd caught Aunt Ruth with the plumber.

"We talked about . . . you know," she finally mumbled. "Stuff."

"Oh, God, no," I said.

"What?"

"You talked about *him*, didn't you? That's what took five hours. *Him*."

She laughed. Now her face was the color of the tomato sauce at Don Vito's.

"What's so funny?" I demanded.

"*You* are," she said. She stood up, wincing a little and massaging her stomach. "I need an Alka Seltzer. But you know what, Tell-It-to-Naomi? You're going to be a great advice columnist. You definitely don't need any help from me. You're wise beyond your years. You see the truth." She laughed once more, then patted my shoulder and waddled out of the room.

I watched her go.

I didn't just feel uncomfortably full anymore. I felt ill. She might as well have pinned an I LOVE JOEL NEWBURY button to her sweater. At this point, she wasn't even trying to hide it from me. And that was . . . well, it was unacceptable.

It was bad enough seeing Mr. Horn-Rimmed Glasses in the halls every day. It was *worse* knowing that he was taking credit (or at least partial credit) for editing a column he didn't even think I wrote. But having to deal with him if he and my sister got back together?

No. That wouldn't happen. That couldn't.

So my mission would have to change. It could no longer be only anti–Zeke Beck. It would also have to be anti–Joel Newbury. Which was where the snag arose. Because, yes, they were both schmucks—but they were two very different *kinds* of schmucks. For example, I doubted Joel Newbury would ever try to read Naomi's palm. Likewise, I doubted Zeke Beck would ever shave his head.

Although . . . Zeke *had* referenced Dalí. He *was* pretentious. And there was no doubt that he'd fondle Celeste Fanucci's butt in public if he had half a chance. Come to think of it, he and Mr. Creaky Leather had something else in common: they both treated me as if I were a five-year-old. What was their problem, anyway? Sure, maybe I didn't have any facial hair. Maybe I looked closer to twelve than fifteen. But that was no—

Wait a second.

There was no reason to get so worked up. This was no snag. No, my mission would be easier now. I should *thank* Naomi. It was all coming together: I wouldn't use the column to spread an anti-Zeke or anti-Joel message; I would use it to spread an anti-*schmuck* message. I would use it to rail against *all* the guys who put on ridiculous airs and acts—*all* the guys who treated skinny sophomores like kindergarteners for the sole purpose of looking mature in front of a chick they wanted to hook up with. I would use it to rail against phonies in general. Every single afternoon I would come home and mine the list of e-mails for three perfect—

"Dave?"

Aunt Ruth was standing in the door. She, too, was clutching her stomach.

"What's up?" I said.

"What have you and your sister been doing in here?" she moaned.

"What do you mean?"

"You've been spending so much time on the computer. You're not running one of these Internet scams, are you?"

I laughed. "Excuse me?"

"Did you see the *Times* magazine the other day?"

"Uh . . . no. Why?"

"There was an article about a boy your age who posed as a doctor on the Internet," Aunt Ruth said. "A medical doctor. People believed him. He gave hundreds of people all sorts of phony advice. And his poor victims! Some of them were really sick. One lady had gout. Her left foot swelled to the size of a melon. The boy was caught and sent to jail for years. He was tried as an adult."

I rolled my eyes. "Aunt Ruth, come on."

"What?"

"Do you really think Naomi and I would run an Internet scam?"

She smiled. "I guess not."

"Okay, then."

"So why don't you come out and have some dessert with us?"

"Dessert? I can't even *walk*."

"Well, at least turn on another light. You'll go blind. And don't work so hard. You're too young to be up working so late at night." She plodded back to the kitchen.

I glanced at the computer.

It wasn't that late. It wasn't even ten. Besides, I had to work *now,* while my new mission was still fresh in my mind. I had to pick three random e-mails—one for the column and two to be polite, as Naomi had suggested.

Technically speaking, the "work" I had to do involved giving people advice on the Internet under a phony name.

It's funny how life turns out sometimes. Yeah. It can be a real crack-up.

I just hoped none of the kids at Roosevelt had gout.

Chapter Twelve ▬▬▬▬▬

Time: 7:12 pm

Subject: cow-sized thighs, no life

dear naomi,

hello, remember me? I'm B.O.Z. from the other day. I
also mentioned in a separate e-mail that my
boyfriend smells. (sorry if I'm overloading your
server, but I have nothing better to do. I TOLD you I
have no life. ☺) anyway, you might think that if I
have a boyfriend, that necessarily means i have a
life, right? boyfriend = life. FAT CHANCE! and I
really DO mean "fat chance," because I am FAT, and if
I dump my boyfriend I probably won't have another
CHANCE to go out with anybody. in addition to having
a beard of zits and cow-sized thighs, I am also
mildly insecure. and okay, my boyfriend smells and
has the IQ of a nail clipper, but he's mine. what do
I do? HELP!

eagerly awaiting your reply,

b.o.z.

Dear Whoever You Are,

First things first: I refuse to call you B.O.Z. I
know you are exaggerating your facial condition. How
do I know? Because I, too, believed that I had a
beard of zits when I was your age.

I also believed that I had cow-sized thighs.

In fact, I believed I was so ugly that I was pretty
much invisible to anyone I cared to be visible to.
And now I know better.

Here's a bit of tough advice: get over your insecurity.
It'll be hard, and it will take time, but don't worry:
you can always write to me if you have trouble. ☺

***

I can tell that you are a great catch just from
reading your e-mail—and THAT is what matters. You are
smart. You are funny. You are the s***.

If your boyfriend can't see that, it's HIS problem.

Now about your boyfriend . . .

It sounds to me like you'd better have a talk with
him—soon. (Especially if he smells!) I get the
feeling you're letting him walk all over you only
because you're scared of being alone.

This is a natural feeling. But just as BOYFRIEND does
not = LIFE, NATURAL does not always = HEALTHY. This

is particularly true when it comes to your own fear.
That pesky emotion can make us human beings do pretty
silly things.

So stand up for yourself. Be strong. And if your
smelly boyfriend can't deal with that, maybe you'd be
better off without him. Breaking up is a scary thing,
but sometimes it's the best thing.

Good luck,
Naomi

P.S. If you write in again as B.O.Z., I won't answer.

* * *

Time: 7:13 pm
Subject: another paranoid rambling note from FONY

Dear Naomi,

So, you really are a genius. This is good to know.
Your last e-mail solved a lot of my problems, but now
I have a whole set of new ones. That's life though,
isn't it?

I guess I'll just stick to the A-B-C format, since it
seems to work pretty well. . . . A) Is it normal for
inside jokes to include numerous references to Satan?
Is that a New York thing? B) Have you ever had that
dream where you fly? I'm serious. I know it sounds
dumb, and everybody's supposed to have it. But when I
do, I really feel like I'm flying and sometimes in
the dream I know I'm dreaming. But it doesn't stop.

I'm still flying—usually over my old home. It makes
me sad. C) If you're in a new school/city/life, do
you think it's better to make friends first, or to
get a boyfriend first?

Please respond to one or all. . . .

FONY

P.S. You were right about A) mullets, B) the falafel
guy on 20th and 5th, AND C) Dr. Seuss. You rule.

***

Dear FONY,
A) I am not a genius. I once tried to make scrambled
eggs in the microwave. True story.

B) In my experience, as far as inside jokes go—
whether they involve the Prince of Darkness or not—
the people who tell them in front of strangers are
generally doing one of three things (I'm going to
deviate from A-B-C here and go to 1-2-3):

1) They want to prove how cool they are, because they
feel insecure for some reason. 2) They've just been
reminded of something funny that only their close
friends would understand, so making the joke was a
natural and innocent reflex—like kicking when you're
tapped on the knee. 3) They want to be friends with
you, and they want YOU to be in on their inside
jokes, and this is their way of inviting you into
their scene without having to explain themselves up
front, which is always awkward.

I hope that makes sense. And this isn't a complete list. There might be a hundred other reasons why somebody would make an inside joke about Satan in front of you. (Devil worship, maybe? ☺) My advice to you: if you like them and it happens again, just ask them to tell you what they're talking about. If they are genuinely cool people, they'll let you in on it. If not, they're probably not worth your time anyway.

C) Yes, I've had the dream where I fly. I read somewhere that dreaming about flying gives you a sense of control. You usually have it when you're under a lot of pressure. (Okay, I admit it: I just looked that up two seconds ago.) Makes sense: you just moved. Plus, your old house is in your dream. You miss it. Crazy dreams are normal, FONY. I once dreamed I was Lenny Kravitz. (If you ever tell anyone that, you're in big trouble!!) Have fun with them, but don't put too much stock in them. . . .

D) Okay. Your Letter C, my Letter D. The friend/boyfriend issue is a tough one. I can't really answer that. I don't think anyone can. Obviously, it's best when your boyfriend IS your friend, and vice versa. Just trust your instincts—I know you have good ones! I will say this: some people (not most!) do try to take advantage of newcomers in slimy ways. Unfortunately, that's just the nature of the world we live in. So be careful. . . .

And no, YOU rule.
Naomi

* * *

Time: 7:14 pm

Subject: PAPA SAY YOU ARE EVIL

NAOMI!

PAPA GOES IN HOSPITAL THAT IS ST VINCENT'S FOR ALMOST
A WEEK. I AM SAD. MAMA IS YET IN PAU. I HAVE NO
FRIENDS. PAPA SAY I NEED NO FRIENDS IN AMERICA
BECAUSE AMERICANS THINK ONLY OF ONESELFS. THEY DO
NOT KNOW HOW TO BE FRIENDS. I SAY THAT IS NOT TRUE! I
TELL HIM ABOUT YOU AND YOUR DR. SEUSS! I SHOULD
LIKE TO BE EXAMINED BY THIS SEUSS! HE IS A WISE
DOCTOR! PAPA SAY YOU ARE AMERICAN THAT IS TO SAY
YOU ARE EVIL. I TELL HIM YOU ARE NOT AMERICAN.
YOU ARE ONLY NAOMI. NOBODY IS NOBODY BUT ONESELF. I
FEAR THAT MAKES NOT SENSE? IT IS DIFFICULT TO
TELL. I TRY TO BE A GOOD DAUGHTER I SLEEP AT HOSPITAL
THAT IS ST. VINCENT'S EVERY FRIDAY AND SATURDAY.
PAPA HAS BEEN ACCUSED BY A NURSE OF SEXUAL
HARASSMENT. THIS IS A BIG TERM, NO? I LOOK IT UP.
SEXUAL IS <<OF OR RELATING TO SEX OR TO RELATIONS
BETWEEN THE SEXES>>. HARASSMENT IS <<TROUBLE
OR ANNOY REPEATEDLY OR MAKE REPEATED ATTACKS
ON AN ENEMY OR OPPONENT>> AS A NOUN. PAPA GRABBED A
NURSE WHO IS FLESHY AS A JOKE. THE NURSE DID NOT
AGREE THAT THE JOKE WAS COMIC. I AGREE WITH NURSE.
NOW PAPA IS MAD TO ME. HOW? I KEEP IT REAL. WORD TO
YOUR MOTHER.

SINCERELY YOURS,

HOSPITAL GIRL

*　*　*

Dear Hospital Girl,

You keep telling me you "keep it real." I have to ask you: is this true? As you say, it is difficult to tell. Because if your e-mails are pranks, they are NOT "comic."

However, since I am not American or evil, but only Naomi, I will give you the benefit of the doubt. I will assume that you are who you claim to be—and not, for instance, somebody who runs the lit club, who drinks coffee on 4th and A, and who thinks advice columns are lame.

Sound familiar? If not, good.

So . . .

I am sorry about your dad. Believe it or not, I can relate. My own father was an alcoholic. So I know that this is a tough situation for you. Are you in touch with your mother? It's important for you to have support, to have somebody to talk to about this. It's never easy. There are no simple solutions. But you aren't alone.

And I will say this: your dad is wrong. Not all Americans are bad news. Some of them can actually be very good friends. They're out there. If you make the effort, I know you'll find them.

He was also wrong to sexually harass his nurse. Sexual harassment is NEVER cool. It's not a joke. It's pretty much—well, EVIL, as you would say. It's doubly evil that he sexually harassed a woman who is

trying to take care of him. You should tell him so.
Even if he does get "mad to" you.

By the way, it's "mad AT" you.

Oh—and one more thing: in recent years "word to your
mother" has been shortened to just plain "word." At
least, I think it has.

Feel free to ask me any questions you want about
slang. I will be sure to give you a variety of wrong
and outdated answers.

Catch you on the flip side, Hospital Girl
—Naomi

P.S. Do not use "catch you on the flip side" in conversation unless you happen to be talking to one of
the original cast members of *Superfly*.

* * *

It was a toss-up between B.O.Z. and FONY, but I wanted to go with
B.O.Z. I convinced Naomi that it was the right call. If we gave FONY
two columns in a row—especially the first two—the other readers
might think "Naomi" was ignoring their e-mails. (Which we were. But
running a sophisticated Internet scam means tricking people.)

First thing Friday morning, Naomi forwarded the e-mails B.O.Z.
and I had exchanged to Joel so the daily installments of "Tell It to
Naomi!" could start running that afternoon.

I'd had a secret reason for picking B.O.Z, of course. I was hoping
that some of my advice about her boyfriend would make my sister
start thinking twice about *her* budding romance—or rekindled romance, or whatever the hell it was.

I'd officially embarked on my anti-schmuck mission. I'd taken the first step.

I knew I wouldn't accomplish it overnight. But I had Hope.

And as for Hospital Girl . . . I didn't even bother sharing *that* little exchange with Naomi. I knew I didn't want it printed in the school paper. Still, I have to admit I was curious. Was Hospital Girl for real? The more I thought about it, the less I hoped so. If she actually existed, she was in serious trouble. I kept feeling twinges of remorse. Maybe I'd been too harsh. What if it was true? I had no business pretending to be "Naomi" to a friendless Algerian with a dying alcoholic father. It put me up there in Evil Land with that kid from the *Times* magazine. Better just to skip over the truly disturbing e-mails. Right. Better to keep it light. Acne, smelly boyfriends, fat thighs—that stuff I could handle. (Sort of, I hoped.)

Besides, Hospital Girl was most likely a fraud. Sure. She was Olga Romanoff. Or *somebody* . . . in which case, I hadn't been harsh enough. For all I knew, I'd scared her off. Maybe she wouldn't write in again.

Although . . .

Friday at school, a part of me wished she would. And this was troubling, because it meant that either a) I got a kick out of reading horribly grim BS, or b) I enjoyed wallowing in my own guilt. *Yikes.* Was I a masochist? Was *I* truly disturbed? What did Papa and his "banana hammock briefs" have to do with my mission, anyway? Nothing. So why could I only think about running home and reading the new batch of e-mails—Hospital Girl's included?

Actually, I knew the answer. It was because I'd become Clark Kent again.

For the second time in a row, everybody was talking about the column I'd written. Everybody but me. Once again, I trudged from class to class alone. Once again, I stole glances at various people, wondering which one was FONY or B.O.Z. or the guy whose shorty thought her hooters were too damn small. Once again, I pictured Cheese at *his* school—holding court over his clones, the way Olga Romanoff held court over her bevy of lit-club chicks.

I am a loser.

The sorrier I felt for myself, the angrier I became with myself. It was ridiculous. I *knew* it was. If I wanted to snap out of the "Bad Funk" and depart the town of Loserville, Population: Dave, I had to make a move. I had to break my pact with Cheese, just as Cheese had broken it. I had to stop treating school as a job. I had to follow my own advice—to get out there and mix and mingle, to move beyond the world of "Hey, what's up?"

Moments after the final bell rang, I saw my chance.

I was hurrying out the big double doors with the rest of the mob when a girl at the bottom of the steps caught my eye. She was a sophomore . . . Karen Wallace. She'd been in my chemistry class last year, along with Jed Beck.

She stood on tiptoe craning her neck. She was obviously waiting for someone.

She didn't have a beard of zits—not even close—but she had a few here and there. And while she wasn't fat, she wasn't a stick, either. She was holding a school paper. (Ergo, she might be a fan of "Tell It to Naomi!" and maybe even somebody who wrote in.) And she was wearing green pants. They looked like they were made of velour or velvet.

She could be B.O.Z, I thought.

Plus, the way she waved at her friends as they passed by—smiling apologetically, possibly not wanting to offend them because she was waiting for someone else (her smelly boyfriend?)—she *could* be, right? She radiated the same humorous, consciously insecure vibe that B.O.Z. did.

I hesitated when I reached her step.

She glanced at me.

I couldn't muster the courage to speak. I waited for the crowd to clear.

"Yeah?" she asked finally.

"I . . . uh, I just noticed you're, um . . . you're wearing pale green pants," I said.

Her face soured.

Now the vibe was different. It wasn't so much B.O.Z. anymore. It was closer to a thug in a rap video or an armed felon.

"*Please,*" she said with a sneer. "Don't even try it."

"Try what?"

"That same lame-ass line everybody else has tried," she said.

"Oh . . . that," I said.

"Yeah, *that*. Anything else?"

"I guess not," I said. "Have a nice day."

"My day will be a whole lot nicer once this conversation is over."

"Gotcha."

I continued on down the stairs to the sidewalk. If I'd needed any more proof that I was a loser . . . Nope. Not a whole lot of ambiguity there, at least as far as Roosevelt was concerned. But I'd just gotten proof of something else, too, something I'd suspected all along: the students here weren't just meatheaded; they were stuck-up jerks. Who the hell did Karen Wallace think she was, anyway? A supermodel? I wasn't *interested* in her. She was chubby and had pimples. I didn't even want to be friends with her—or with anyone else at this stupid school.

No. I had plenty of friends. *Real* friends.

They were all waiting for me at home, inside Naomi's computer.

Chapter Thirteen

"Dave! There you are."

I'd forgotten I'd been worried about my sister's mental health in recent days. But when I arrived home that Friday, standing in her doorway, it all came flooding back. She'd cleaned. Or maybe the word was *reorganized*. Her room wasn't exactly neater. It looked more as if it had been turned inside out. The garbage had been bagged, the newspapers had been stacked—but all her drawers were open, and most of her clothes were sprawled in haphazard piles across her bed. The shades were still drawn, too.

"So where have you been?" she said.

"See, there's this place called school," I said. "It's where I go to learn stuff. You might have heard of it."

"Ha, ha, funnyman. It's almost six o'clock."

Worry began to turn to deep concern. "Uh . . . Naomi?" I said. "It's not even four-thirty."

"Really?" Her eyes narrowed. She marched right past me, down the hall into the kitchen. "I lost my watch," she muttered under her breath. "I just checked the . . . " Her voice dropped off. She laughed. "Oh! The clock in the kitchen is dead. No wonder. You know, you'd think with their raises, Mom and Aunt Ruth could spring for a new clock."

I stared at her as she sauntered back into her room.

"*You* haven't started experimenting with drugs, have you?" I asked.

Naomi began to examine a pair of black pants hanging over her desk chair. "Dave, I'm not in the mood right now. I'm feeling a little crazy."

"Yeah, I gathered that. But if you want to see what time it is, you can turn on your computer. There's a clock on it. Or you can open your blinds. You vampires may not know this, but at this time of year, the sun at four-thirty is higher—"

"Speaking of sun, what's up with Cheese, anyway?" Naomi interrupted.

I frowned. "What?"

"He called me son. I saw him in the lobby yesterday, and he said—and I quote verbatim—'Naomi! What's the dilly, son?' The *dilly*."

"You saw him yesterday?"

"Yeah, before we went to Don Vito's," she said absently. "He was with some kid who was carrying a guitar case . . . but look." She grabbed the pants off the back of the chair and held them up to herself. "What do you think?"

"Wait," I said. "You say that Cheese—"

"Just look," she said.

Suddenly she broke out with a grisly, toothpaste-model smile. I flinched.

"Do you think this is too close to what I wore the other night when I went to meet Brian?" she asked. She kept smiling as she spoke, so I could barely understand her. It sounded as if her jaw were wired shut. "I only have that one suit," she added. "And all my nice pants are black."

Life had ceased to make any sense. I felt as if *I* were on drugs. "Naomi, you have to slow down," I said. "I've had a bad day."

She stamped her foot. "*Da-a-ave*," she whined. "Just tell me."

"What, if they look the same? Sure. I don't know. Who cares? But you say that Cheese was with—"

"You should care," Naomi interrupted. She tossed the pants aside. "As a chick."

"As a . . . what?"

"You heard me." She flashed a wry grin. "You're a female advice columnist now. You have to think like a chick. You said you could, Dave. Remember?" She sighed and began to rummage through the clothes on her bed. "Seriously, listen up. Chicks are gonna ask you about this. Clothing is of supreme importance. You *can't* wear the same thing twice. Not if you just met somebody and you're meeting that same somebody again. It doesn't matter how much time has passed between your first and second meeting. It could be a day, a week, or a year. If you're a chick, you have to wear something different. Remember that. Guys never—"

The phone rang.

"Screen it," Naomi said.

"Why?"

"All right, fine—answer it." She snatched up a blue dress and hurried out into the hall again. "But if it's for me, I'm not here. . . ." She slammed the bathroom door behind her.

"You aren't?"

"I have to get ready!" she shouted.

It was official: Naomi had lost her mind. She never screened calls. She *ran* for calls. She *dove* for calls. What if it was the guy from the *New Yorker*? What if he'd changed his mind and wanted to hire her to infiltrate the seamy world of Mafia-controlled waste management? I hoped it was that guy. Then maybe she'd realize what a freak she was being.

I darted for the phone in the kitchen.

"Hello?"

"Oh, hi!" a girl replied. "Is Naomi there, please?"

Whoever it was, she definitely sounded too young to work for a high-powered magazine. I peered down the hall to the closed bathroom door.

"No, she isn't right now," I said. "Can I take a message?"

"Hey, is this Dave?"

"Uh . . . yeah? Who's this?"

"It's Celeste Fanucci. You know, from school?"

* * *

A quick aside:

When I was six, Mom and Aunt Ruth took me to Coney Island against my will. I'd never expressed any desire to go. Riding an ancient roller coaster called the Cyclone in the far reaches of Brooklyn sounded terrifying, especially since Cheese's dad had recently taken us to the Brooklyn Children's Museum and warned us that—contrary to what we saw—most neighborhoods outside Manhattan were "not safe for kids."

I didn't have a choice, though. According to the Laws of Mom and Aunt Ruth, a day at Coney Island was a rite of passage, like a bar mitzvah. Naomi had gone; now it was my turn. To make matters worse, I had to endure this rite of passage alone, without Naomi *or* Cheese. "Cheese will fidget too much on the subway," Mom had insisted. "It's an hour's ride each way, at least."

Anyway, when I *saw* the Cyclone, with its peeling paint and rickety wood, and heard the agonized screams of the people strapped into the cars . . . well, I turned green. I nearly vomited right there at the amusement park entrance. Mom and Aunt Ruth were too caught up in nostalgia to notice. "See that, Dave? Nobody makes wooden roller coasters like that anymore. Probably because metal is so much sturdier than wood."

Then I did vomit.

Mom and Aunt Ruth must have felt bad, because they turned around and took me right home. It wasn't even eleven in the morning, but I got straight into bed and hid under the covers until dinnertime.

The point of this story?

Now you have an understanding of how I felt when Celeste called.

* * *

"Hello?" Celeste said.

"Yeah—hi. I'm still here. Sorry."

"Are you okay? You don't sound so great."

"Oh, I'm fine," I said, my voice cracking. I had no idea why I was so jittery. I was never this jittery when I saw Celeste in school. On the other hand, I expected to see her there. Here, she'd caught me completely off guard. "How—um, how are you?"

She laughed. "I'm okay. So your sister's not home, huh?"

"No! I mean . . . no. She's out with a friend."

"Oh," Celeste said. "Well, I just wanted to ask her advice about something. It's not a big deal, you know? See, I'm going to this open-mike thing tonight? It's at a bar called the Spiral Lounge? Have you heard of it? On Avenue B? They have this thing—like, one Friday a month they let anybody who wants to, get up and perform? And you don't have to be twenty-one? And I figured since I heard that a bunch of kids from school were going . . . ?"

Whenever Celeste spoke for more than a few seconds at a time, I couldn't listen. Her words floated right into the ether. My mind raced to a thousand different places, dreaming up madcap, romantic scenarios, imagining the conversations we *should* have been having. And this brand-new habit of mysteriously ending every single sentence as if it were a question . . . that didn't help, either. It gave her speech a musical, hypnotic quality—like when you hear somebody running their fingers across a harp from the low strings to the high, again and again.

". . . was wondering if it might make a good story?"

"Huh?" I said.

She giggled. "I'm sorry. My fault! Like you care about a dumb story I want to write about an open-mike night!"

Blood rushed to my face. "No, no. I mean, it sounds . . . cool."

109

"Really?"

"Yeah."

"So, Dave," she said, suddenly serious.

I swallowed. "Mm-hmm?"

"Can you please tell me if your sister writes the column?" Celeste whispered. "I won't tell a soul. I promise."

"I—I—" My heart thumped. I should have screened this call.

Celeste giggled again. "I know. It's not fair of me to ask. But listen, if she gets back anytime soon, tell her I called, okay? It's not, like, a big deal or anything. But if she could give me some feedback about this idea, that would be great. I'd feel better about going to Mr. Newbury with a story idea if I know that Naomi had given it, like, the thumbs-up."

I regained some of my composure. "No problem," I said.

"And if you're not doing anything tonight, you should come check it out. Have you ever been? To the Spiral Lounge, I mean?"

"Um . . ." I hadn't, but it was kind of ironic she'd asked.

When Cheese and I first decided to become rock stars—the very same night Mom and Aunt Ruth had given me my electric guitar for Hanukkah—we hatched a plan to perform at open-mike nights at the Spiral Lounge. It would be step one on our rise to glory. After all, we knew that they let anyone play, even teenagers with zero talent. And we would show them zero talent. Oh, yes. We would tear the roof off the dump with our unique brand of post-Zeppelin, post-Strokes, post-*music* rock 'n' roll.

Obviously, we never believed that this would actually happen. Even at that early stage we knew we were a band in names only. What mattered was talking about it. And laughing about it. And ragging on anybody who actually *would* get up and—

"Okay, so maybe I'll see you there?" Celeste asked.

I laughed feebly. "Sure," I said.

"Oh, and remember Ezekiel? I introduced you to him the other day? He's going to perform! Solo acoustic. Have you ever heard him play? He's, like, a serious musician. His stuff is like unplugged Nirvana meets DJ Shadow. He sets up sequencing and loops with a laptop, then runs it through the soundboard and plays along to himself on acoustic guitar—"

"I gotta go, Celeste."

"Okay, bye! If I don't—"

I hung up.

For several seconds I held on to the phone.

I held on so hard my knuckles turned white.

And then . . .

I relaxed. I let go.

Miraculously, I *smiled*.

The spell Celeste Fanucci had put on me was finally broken.

What did I care if she was going to see the Palm Reader play? Celeste Fanucci was a fool. A ditz. *She* was a loser. It was a good thing I *hadn't* screened the call, because now I knew for sure that my crush on her was . . . well, for want of a stronger word, wrong. Celeste may have looked like the ideal woman. But she wasn't. No way.

Which meant that I was free again.

And this time, freedom was just what I craved.

I glanced back down the hall at the bathroom. The faucet was running. I wondered if Naomi had overheard our conversation. Not that it mattered. I'd tell her that Celeste had called as soon as she was out. A crazy idea was beginning to form in my brain. Or maybe . . .

Maybe it was the sanest idea I'd had in a long time.

What if Cheese and I buried our stupid hatchet? What if he and I actually *did* perform at the open-mike night at the Spiral Lounge? Just the two of us? *Tonight?* True, we'd never played together. True, we didn't know how. But what if we got up onstage—and I thrashed on my out-of-tune guitar, and Cheese actually did dive into a vat of gravy—and we were so sublimely ridiculous that we made every other performer look ridiculous by extension?

What if we went and made an anti–open mike statement?

It would be beautiful. We would rag on all the so-called serious musicians, live and in concert, no less. We really could call it "The

Mind Is a Terrible Thing." It wouldn't be so much *music* as one big *gag* . . . a demented piece of performance art.

That would be cutting-edge. *That* would be cash money in the bank, as Cheese would say.

Even better, I bet Celeste would think it was funny. (Not that I cared what she thought now that I was free of her spell.) Better than that, I bet Zeke Beck wouldn't think it was funny at all. And maybe Cheese himself would realize that being in a nonjoke band wasn't all it was cracked up to be. . . .

Without a second thought I dashed out of the apartment and hurtled down the stairs. I laughed out loud. This was great. Cheese would *love* this: me, showing up like old times—as if nothing had happened, as if I didn't care that he'd made new friends (which I shouldn't, anyway)—and hitting him up with this ingenious scheme. . . .

"Hello?" I pounded on the old familiar door of 2F. "Cheese? Anybody home?"

Footsteps approached. The door opened a crack.

It was Cheese's father. He had a cordless phone shoved against one ear. *Oops.* I'd interrupted him. I knew he worked from home sometimes—although doing what, I'd never quite figured out. I don't think Cheese knew for sure, either. It definitely involved yelling at people because I could hear him sometimes as I passed their apartment.

"Hi, Dave," he said, covering the mouthpiece with one hand. "What's up?"

I smiled sheepishly. "I was just looking for . . ."

Mr. Harrison shook his head. "He's at band practice right now."

"Band practice?"

"I know: that's what *I* said." Mr. Harrison laughed. "Haven't you heard? Our Mr. Cheese fancies himself a rock star now."

"Oh." I tried to laugh, too. The sound died somewhere in my chest.

"I'll tell him you stopped by," Mr. Harrison said. "He won't be home until tomorrow, though. He's spending the night at Mike's."

"Oh. Mike's. Okay. Um . . . thanks."

He closed the door.

I turned and headed home.

Funny. It seemed to take about a thousand times longer to climb back up the stairs than it had to come down.

Chapter Fourteen

The weekend was . . .

I'll put it this way: if I'd thought that performing onstage with Cheese would somehow transform me, that it would be a cathartic ritual on par with an exorcism—terrifying, euphoric, an extreme experience—I learned that such experiences, like "the worst things in the world," sneak up on you in ways you can't foresee. You can't *plan* for them.

I'd assumed that the weekend would suck. And in some respects it did. But I finally rode the Cyclone. My head spun with fear and joy. I laughed hysterically; I nearly cried a few times; I almost screamed once or twice . . . and all without ever leaving Naomi's room. Without leaving her *chair*. Because I got exactly what I'd wished for at school on Friday. I got to spend time with my new friends.

I came to know them pretty well, too.

✳ ✳ ✳

Time: 4:53 pm
Subject: the artist formerly known as B.O.Z.

dear naomi,

okay, so I'm changing my name to s.o.m.b. it stands

for Sick Of My Boyfriend. I still think B.O.Z. fits
me better, but . . . crap! there I go again. I know
I'm not supposed to put myself down so much. but I
can't help it. my mom says I use self-deprecating
humor as a defense mechanism. Maybe she's right.
ARRGH!!! you want to know what sucks? i can't talk
about these problems with my friends. Because even
though I am fat and ugly and have NO LIFE, I am also
somehow the center of our little group. sound
impossible? Here's my trick: I never show any
weakness. I mean I do, but I always make a joke out
of it. or i get mad. But I never get mad at my
boyfriend. only at my friends, who are never NEARLY
as heinous as he is . . .

* * *

Time: 5:03 pm
Subject: I SHOULD LIKE TO LEARN SLANGS

NAOMI!

I DO NOT KNOW THAT I UNDERSTAND YOUR PAST
CORRESPONDENCE. YOU SAY I DO NOT KEEP IT REAL! I AM
SAD IF YOU DO NOT AGREE WITH ME. YOU ARE VERY KIND
WHAT YOU SAY ABOUT SUPPORT. YOU ARE MY SUPPORT. I AM
SAD ABOUT YOUR PAPA AND ALCOHOL. ST. VINCENT'S DOES
NOT MAKE MY PAPA LEAVE BECAUSE HE GAVE HIS SORRY TO
THE NURSE. I AM HAPPY! WHAT IS A SUPER FLY? MANY OF
THE SLANGS I LEARN ARE FROM A VIDEO I FIND IN A
MARKET A LONG TIME PAST IN ALGIERS. IT IS A PIRATE
VIDEO. THAT IS TO SAY IT IS AGAINST THE LAW. IT IS
OF A SHOW THAT IS YO! MTV RAPS. IT HAS A LOT OF DEF
BANDS, SUCH AS BEASTIE BOYS, PUBLIC ENEMY, FRESH

PRINCE, AND HUMPTY HUMP. IT IS ILL IF ILL IS GREAT.
PERHAPS YOU SHOULD LIKE TO SEE IT . . .

* * *

Time: 5:22 pm
Subject: too late for that mullet?

Dear Naomi,

Watch out: FONY's mixing it up this time! She's
scrapping the A-B-C format!

Call me crazy but I like to live dangerously.

I'm also very funny, as you can see. What else can I
tell you? I told you about one of my dreams. But I
dream even when I'm awake. Every minute of every day
I have crazy dreams about people I say hi to. I dream
entire futures involving our interconnected lives:
picnics, vacations, reunions, and all. And then the
strangers are gone down the hall, into a classroom,
and on with reality-and the dreams go with them. So I
say hi to someone else. And it starts again.

Is that normal? If not, maybe Jersey IS the answer . . .

This isn't a complete list, by the way. I received 162 e-mails that
weekend. These are just the ones I opened first.

* * *

By 9 p.m. Friday, I was exhausted. Sitting in front of a computer
for four straight hours can do that to you. So can rage. And I was

pretty full of rage that night. It wasn't because Cheese was spending the night at Mike's, either—or because Celeste Fanucci was watching Zeke Beck's Solo Acoustic Tape-Loop Crap-Fest while I sat at home. It was because I kept thinking, *Naomi's right. I* am *a chick.* I wasn't just "feminine." The kids who wrote in believed that I was Naomi. I answered them as Naomi. Which made me Naomi.

Ergo, I was a chick.

But as I discovered, rage seems to have the same effect as crack. It pumps you up full of insanity and venom, and then it wears off fast—leaving a big, empty hole.

(Just to be clear, no, I've never tried crack. I mean: *crack?* I've never tried *any* drug. Not even bus fumes. But drug metaphors were on my mind because Friday at assembly, the administration forced the entire sophomore class to sit through one of those ridiculous *Say No!* videos. This one gave new meaning to the expression *old school.* I'm sure Naomi had to watch the exact same one when *she* was a sophomore. It was all muffled and grainy, full of bizarre references to things I'd never heard of, like Reaganomics. On the other hand, it did give me a good idea of what Hospital Girl's pirated *Yo! MTV Raps* tape must have looked like.)

Anyway, I was too angry on Friday to keep scrolling through the e-mails. I shut down Naomi's computer and crawled into bed. I didn't even bother to write anyone back. Which was a good thing. Lord knows what I would have said.

Saturday morning, though, something began to change.

I wasn't so angry anymore. I began to fill the big, empty hole.

It started with FONY.

I crept back into Naomi's room—she was still sleeping—and reread the e-mail. And for the first time, I didn't think about any mission or hidden agenda. (I admit I was groggy.) I didn't even really think about what I was doing. I just tried to figure out how to help this random freshman girl, this stranger, for the simple reason that I liked her. Or what I read of her, anyway.

And that was when I realized: FONY *doesn't need any help at all. She's as normal as they come.*

If dreaming the impossible about random strangers was a problem, we *all* needed help. Or at least I did. I dreamed the impossible every time I saw Celeste Fanucci. And what about Karen Wallace? I'd dreamed she was the artist formerly known as B.O.Z. I'd gone so far as to *act* on that dream. *Jeez.* Maybe it *was* a problem. If your dream life started getting mixed up with your real life, it could be pretty confusing. Worse, it could be embarrassing. Maybe I just didn't know what "normal" was. Maybe *that* was the problem. All I really knew for sure was the jumble of absurdity inside my own head. Karen Wallace *could* be S.O.M.B. She might have just made an assumption about me (namely, that I was a sniveling, horny little weasel), the same way I'd made an assumption about *her*. There was no way I could admit to who I really was, any more than she could. So on some level we had to perpetuate a dream. . . .

I began to type.

I typed that FONY had nothing to worry about. She was new. Dreaming about strangers was a perfectly fine way of coping with *being* a stranger. Sure, it might not be "normal"—but "normal" according to whom? Jerks who were too scared to admit that they've ever felt out of place? Dreaming was positive. It was a lot more positive than pretending to be somebody she wasn't. I knew this from experience. I typed that I understood what it was like to be new, too, because . . . because . . . well, here, I had to stop typing to make something up—

"Dave?"

Naomi was awake.

"Yeah?" I whispered.

She yawned. "What are you doing?"

"Working on the column. Go back to sleep."

"I can't," she groaned. "You're making too much noise."

I glanced over my shoulder. "Sorry. Can you give me five more minutes?"

She pursed her lips. In the dim glow of the monitor, I could see dark circles under her eyes. I wondered when she'd gotten home last night. Nah . . . on second thought, I didn't want to know. She'd been out with Brian Somebody and *him*.

"All right, five minutes," she mumbled. She collapsed back against her pillow. "But I'm gonna talk to Mom and Aunt Ruth about hooking you up with Internet access so you can do this from your room."

"Please do." I turned back to the computer, wriggling my fingers over the keyboard. "It's time they put those raises to good use."

"What's so important, anyway?" Naomi asked. "I mean, what are you writing that can't wait until I get up?"

"Nothing," I said.

"It can't be *nothing*."

I hesitated. "It's something I should have written all along," I said.

"What's that?"

"The truth."

"The *what*?" she cried.

I glanced back at her. "Not *that* truth," I muttered.

"Then what?" She sat up straight, suddenly wide awake. "What truth? I mean it, Dave. What are you writing?"

"It's . . ." I didn't know how to explain myself. I didn't know if I could. "I just want to be honest. There are all kinds of truth."

She glared at me. "All kinds of truth? What's that supposed to mean? You sound like you joined a conspiracy cult. I'm serious, Dave. We have to be really careful here."

"I *know*, Naomi," I groaned. "You think I would tell anyone about what really goes on with the column?"

"No, it's just . . ." She sighed. "No. I'm sorry. I know you wouldn't."

"Okay, then," I said.

"You're right." She settled back down, closing her eyes. "Sorry. And I do hear what you're saying about wanting to be honest. You're great at that. But remember, Dave: there are all kinds of lies, too. People love to tell lies. They *have* to. And you know I speak from experience. . . . " Her lips curled in an odd, melancholy grin. "So be careful, okay?"

"About what?"

Naomi rolled over, settling under the covers. "Just be careful," she said. "You promise?"

"I promise."

"Good. Now finish up and let me sleep."

Chapter Fifteen

Once Naomi was up and out of the room, I scurried back to the computer. I basically stayed put until Sunday—except for when I had to eat and sleep. I opened every single e-mail, too. I *read* every single e-mail, as a matter of fact—all 162—the ludicrous, the profane, the silly, the sad . . . the Cyclone.

That isn't to say I answered all of them.

No, I only ended up answering ones that came from FONY. It started when she wrote back to thank me for my initial reply.

```
You're right. FONY needs to feel "normal"
like a fish needs a bicycle.
HA! Ever heard that one?
```

After that, we fell into a kind of routine. I would be reading a note from some poor girl who'd been dumped, or who'd eaten nothing but a bowl of cereal in the past two days, or who'd suffered a nervous breakdown on a college admissions tour . . . when Naomi's computer would announce (always, it seemed, at the precise moment I couldn't stand to read another excruciating line): "You've got mail."

```
Time: 11:53 am
Subject: diarrhea
```

Why the word <u>diarrhea</u>? Why such an ugly word for any ugly thing? Why not a silly word, so it won't be so embarrassing? Like "snorf" or something? Five letters, tops. "I'm not feeling well today, Dad, I have a little snorf." I'll explain later. My dad's a research scientist.

* * *

Time: 3:18 pm
Subject: DeKalb Avenue????

I just went to Brooklyn. I didn't plan to go, but the subway loudspeakers only broadcast static. Do you have to be from New York to understand what they say? Maybe there was a warning. I don't know. I got on at Union Square. I was supposed to be going underneath downtown, and then I found myself on a bridge over a river going to a place called DeKalb Avenue. But it wasn't so bad. The view over the river = beautiful. Sparkles and skyscrapers and boats. The view on Dekalb Avenue = not so beautiful.

* * *

Time: 5:07 pm
Subject: the person in charge of the rules

Girls LIKE piercing their belly buttons, and you can't blame them. I want to get MINE pierced. Belly buttons are sexy. So why is it a terrible crime not to know all the lyrics to "Oklahoma!" I'll explain later. My dad's a conservative.

That was the pattern, if you could call it that. I'd answer one out of about every three:

```
Hi FONY,

I don't know about the sexy thing. It totally depends
on the belly button. My fifty-year-old aunt's belly
button = not so sexy. And my question to YOU is: Why
is it a crime to exchange Funkadelic's Maggot Brain
for, say, a CD you'd actually want to listen to? I'll
explain later. My mom's a lunatic.
```

Somehow, FONY and I established something—although I don't know if it was a rapport exactly. Not in the traditional sense. It was more like . . . a mutual appreciation for nonsense and stupidity. Whatever it was, it was a lot more enjoyable than trying to figure out how to help a girl who was on the verge of starving herself.

If that sounds a little flip . . . well, I admit, I didn't know how to deal with some of the stuff I read. It was too heavy. I guess I was sort of like S.O.M.B: I had to joke about it; otherwise, I would feel uncomfortable. And yes, I knew I could always tell Naomi about the girls who were in danger, and she could tell Joel, and he could intervene. But the problem was that I didn't *know* who was in danger. How could I? I wasn't a therapist. I wasn't even a psych major. I was a *boy*. I was a *liar*. It was the Hospital Girl conundrum: maybe these kids were exaggerating. Maybe they were flat-out lying, too. I could just picture it: some idiot writes in as a sick prank, claiming that her father is locking her in the basement at night, and Joel Newbury suddenly shows up at her door with the NYPD—in the middle of Dad's birthday party, *when Dad is perfectly innocent and has no idea what's going on.*

No, it was best to trust my first instincts. It was best to skip over the horrific, to stick to the light and fluffy . . . and to leave Naomi out of the whole process.

Technically, I wasn't even working on the column, anyway. I couldn't *print* what went back and forth between FONY and me. I'm sure my sister would agree. It was inane. Some of it was downright moronic, along the lines of the conversations I used to have with Cheese.

As it turned out—luckily—Naomi's involvement never came up. She was out most of the weekend. (Again, I didn't want to think about where.) When she was home, she was usually passed out in bed. (And I didn't want to think about *why*. But as I soon learned, she *could* sleep right through the clackety-clack of the keyboard.)

Mom and Aunt Ruth left me alone, too. They spent most of the weekend buying a new kitchen clock. For sane people, I imagine that buying a clock doesn't require two full days—although, since I don't have any direct experience with the sane, this is just a guess. I do know that Mom and Aunt Ruth expend hundreds of man-hours scouring the city whenever they purchase an electronic device, no matter how basic. They call this "comparison shopping."

So I had the apartment to myself.

Same old, same old, I thought. But this time it was no tragedy. Not even close.

I had FONY all to myself, too.

***

Around dinnertime on Sunday evening, there was a knock on the door.

"Dave?"

"Yeah, Mom?"

"Can I come in?"

"Sure." I stretched and arched my back, wincing. My whole body ached from sitting for so long.

She entered cautiously. "I don't want to interrupt anything."

"No, it's fine," I said. "I could use a break."

"Okay." She eased herself down on Naomi's bed. "Dave . . . ah, I'm a little concerned."

I sighed. "I'm fine, Mom. I just—"

"I know," she interrupted. "Naomi told me all about it."

My heart froze. I whirled and stared at her. "Told you about what?"

"She told me that she's been writing an advice column for your school newspaper."

"She . . . did?"

"Yes, she did. She also told me that you're helping her out. She said you volunteered to help sort through these kids' letters for her. And it sounds like a noble cause. I'm not saying otherwise. It's very thoughtful and considerate of you to help."

Here, Mom raised both her hands—palms out, as if being arrested. This was a favorite gesture of hers. Aunt Ruth used it a lot, too. It meant: *I don't know what you children are up to, and I don't care. Do whatever you want. Just don't be surprised when you end up in hell for all eternity.*

"I'm only saying you might want to reconsider," she said.

I was speechless. I almost started cracking up.

"Mom, there's nothing to worry about," I said. "I'm fine. I enjoy helping Naomi with her advice column. It makes me feel like I'm a part of something. It's good to get involved with extracurricular activities, you know?"

The whole time I spoke, I envisioned giving Naomi a standing ovation. My sister was a genius. A twisted and depraved genius, to be sure—but she'd said it herself yesterday: ". . . *remember, Dave: there are all kinds of lies, too.*" She was absolutely right. Truth and Untruth (just like dream life and real life) could get mixed up in all *sorts* of unexpected ways.

"Helping Naomi with the column is a lot of fun," I added for good measure.

Mom studied my face for a moment. "Okay. Just so long as you're not cooped up in here because you're sad." She hesitated. "I mean, it's not because of Cheese, is it? I don't see him around much anymore. Is there something going on?"

I frowned. "Who said that?"

Mom hesitated. "Somebody who's concerned about you, too."

Anger flashed over me. "Naomi? How does she know?"

"Dave, I'm sorry," Mom said. "Naomi should have come to you first. It isn't fair of me to ask about it, any more than it was fair of her to tell me about it. But . . . your sister's a smart cookie." Mom laughed ruefully. "And as we all know, she can't keep a secret."

I turned back to the computer, seething.

Forget the ovation. For the second time in a very short while, I fantasized about wringing Naomi's neck. She wasn't a genius; she was a *jerk*. She'd figured something out about *me*, about *my friend*—something that was none of her freaking business to begin with—and she'd blabbed. I was half tempted to confess the truth about the column right then and there, just to get back at her.

"Please don't be mad at her, Dave," Mom said quietly. "Okay?"

"Whatever," I grumbled.

"Can I tell you something?" she asked.

I shrugged.

"It's a secret," she said. "You can't tell Naomi. Promise?"

"Mom," I groaned. "I'm not a five-year-old. Can we just drop it?"

"This has nothing to do with your age. Do you know why Aunt Ruth and I bought you a Stratocaster for Hanukkah last year? A white Stratocaster?"

My eyes narrowed. I slowly spun back around in the chair.

"It was because of Naomi," Mom said.

"What do you mean?"

"She was worried about you. She was worried you were having a hard time in school. So she came up with the idea of buying you a guitar. But not just any guitar. She wanted to be sure we got you the exact same kind of guitar Hendrix played at Woodstock. And you know why? You want to know what she said? She said, 'I know Dave. He'll recognize the guitar. And it'll make him really happy because he'll know *we'll* recognize it, too. So it'll be like giving all of us a present. That's the kind of thing he really digs. We can share it.'"

I swallowed.

Man.

I'd had no idea.

A large, uncomfortable lump began to find its way into my throat. It shouldn't have been there. It didn't *belong* there.

"And just so you know, Naomi isn't the only one who's noticed you haven't been yourself lately," Mom murmured.

"Well, what about *her?*" I asked, wanting to change the subject before I made a fool out of myself. "I mean, *she's* one to judge, you know? She's been losing everything lately. Her wallet, her watch . . . She didn't even realize the kitchen clock was broken. What's going on?"

Mom grinned. "Oh, that's an easy one. She's fallen back in love—with that fellow she dated a while ago, the one who teaches at your school. People are always absentminded when they're in love."

The lump abruptly dissolved.

"*What?*"

"So you've noticed too, huh?" she asked.

"She *said* this to you?"

"Not with words. But, yes. She's been saying it to everybody. She's been telling the whole world, don't you think?" Mom raised her eyebrows. "Have you seen the kind of outfits she's been wearing?"

My face grew stony. I didn't even want to think about that question, much less answer it.

"Once in love, always in love," Mom added.

I frowned. Now she sounded as if she were quoting a cheesy romance novel.

"Sorry," Mom said in a faraway voice. "I was just thinking of a letter Jae Hee sent me a long time ago."

Oh, brother, I thought. *Here we go. . . .*

Jae Hee is one of my mom's oldest friends. She *always* sounds like a cheesy romance novel. Or not "sounds"—because I've never heard her speak. Neither has Mom. Their friendship is definitely unique: They've never met in person, and I doubt they ever will. They communicate only by mail. They've never even *called* each other. Jae Hee lives in Seoul. They were randomly assigned to each other as pen pals when they were both sixth graders, and forty years later they're still at it. (Why is a mystery. Mom is blunt to the point of being offensive, whereas Jae Hee has always had a serious penchant for the hokey. She once referred to Naomi and me as Mom's fragile cherubs. Come to think of it, her English has something in common with Hospital Girl's—Jae Hee's is more coherent, obviously—but there's always a certain *off*-ness, a goofy courtesy that native English speakers don't seem to have.)

"It was right after your father died," Mom said.

I stiffened, suddenly rapt with attention.

Mom never mentioned Dad. *Ever.*

"What else did Jae Hee say?"

Mom moaned wistfully. "She said she knew I was sad that he passed away. She said I may have hated your father for what he did to us, and to himself . . . but a part of me would always love him, no matter what. She said true love is like chicken pox. You only get it once, when you're young. It may leave scars—but some of it stays inside you for the rest of your life."

Now I wasn't so rapt anymore.

I leaned back in Naomi's chair.

That was possibly the most ridiculous thing I'd ever heard. *True love is like chicken pox?* Classic Jae Hee: she'd dished out what sounded like a proverb, wise and grandiose—but in reality it meant squat. Not that I should have expected anything more. *She* couldn't impart any insight on Dad. She didn't know any more about him than I did. How could she? She'd never traveled outside South Korea.

"Someday you'll understand," Mom said.

"About what?"

"About chicken pox."

"I've already had it."

"Not like this," she said.

"Hey, Mom? What, um . . ." I wasn't even sure what I wanted to ask. "Why did you keep in touch with Jae Hee? I mean—no, that came out wrong . . . what was it about her that got to you? You know, at first?"

Mom smiled curiously. "What was it that got to me?"

"Yeah. What made you guys become such good friends?"

"Hmm." She looked down at the floor. "That's a good question. I . . . To be honest, I doubt we'd be so close if we'd met face to face as kids. Our backgrounds are so different. It's such a surprise when we do have something in common." She chuckled. "You know, when we first wrote, I had to explain to her what 'Jewish' meant? I guess there aren't a whole lot of Jews in her area of Seoul. . . . I think it's because we haven't met. And we never will. When I write to Jae Hee, I don't have to worry about what she already knows about me. And it works both ways. There are no preconceptions." Mom glanced up at me. "We only know what's on paper."

"I hate to admit this, but you actually made sense to me just now. Sort of," I said.

"I did? I actually made sense to my hip young son?" She beamed and raised a clenched fist over her head. "Rock on!"

I winced. "Please don't ever say that again."

She stepped into the hall. "Dinner's almost ready."

I nearly said something else . . . but no. It was best not to. At that moment I was content with having a new secret. Naomi—despite her obvious faults (blabbing, harboring an undying love for Joel Bald-Head, et cetera)—had shared valuable Wisdom with me.

It was Wisdom that Mom had just confirmed.

"People love to tell lies," Naomi had told me. *"They have to tell lies."*

Only now did I realize that she'd been talking about *us*. About her and me.

Truth and Untruth *could* get mixed up. But the results didn't have to be confusing or catastrophic. On the contrary, certain lies could be even more truthful than Truth itself.

time: 5:45 pm
subject: business

Dear Naomi,

Hi. The Bad Kid, here. First-time writer, longtime
reader. Vital stats: I am a sophomore. I go to a
cruel school that is thinking about making us wear
uniforms. I am devastatingly gorgeous, if your taste
runs toward the thin and hairy. So now that you have
a clear mental image of me, let's get down to
business: What am I supposed to do if my best friend
is pissed because she knows that I have a crush on
her older brother? We've been best friends our entire
lives. Now we don't even talk. It bites.

Rock on—

The Bad Kid

Dear Bad Kid,

Wow. We must be Psychic Friends or something because
believe it or not, I am having the EXACT SAME PROBLEM
with my best friend.

Like you and yours, she and I have known each other
our entire lives. She's always known my older
brother. Recently, I think she's started to have a
little crush on him, too.

Now she acts like I don't even exist. We got in a
stupid fight over nothing—it definitely didn't have
to do with my brother—and now it's like we were never

friends at all. I don't even CARE that she has a crush on my older brother . . .

But enough about me.

My advice? Make the first move. Tell her exactly how you feel. Call her; stop her on the street; show up at her door if you have to—do whatever it takes to get a dialogue started. This won't be easy. The longer you let things slide, the harder it will be. If she's really the best friend you think she is, she'll be grateful.

And for your part, try to understand where SHE's coming from. If she has a crush on your older brother, so what? Chances are she'll grow out of it soon, if she hasn't already. Crushes are fleeting. Best friendships aren't. Remember that.

Rock on with your own bad self & good luck,
Naomi

Chapter Sixteen

A week went by—then two, then three.

The nights grew longer. We celebrated the High Holidays. I watched the Columbus Day parade on TV. The leaves changed color in Central Park.

And chatting with FONY took over completely.

It consumed me. Everything else began to fade. *Everything.* School, the fight with Cheese, Mom and Aunt Ruth's moaning—even, in some ways, "Tell It to Naomi!" FONY would send me a stupid three-line e-mail. And I would reply. And then we would be off . . . and we wouldn't stop until one of us had to—usually when Mom and Aunt Ruth dragged me away to dinner. (Often by force.)

We never chatted about anything worthwhile. Oh, no. Not once. A dozen girls would write in about how depressed they were; FONY would tell me about how she'd just discovered the Three-Dollar Theater in midtown.

It's the greatest bargain ever, except for the stink!

And I would write that I agreed. Except for the time I went to see *The Pianist* and inexplicably found myself watching a 1988 Charlie Sheen caper instead, dubbed in Spanish.

And she would reply that I was lucky. The last time *she* went, an old woman fell asleep on her shoulder. The drool stains still wouldn't come out in the wash.

And so on and so on and so on . . .

That sort of exchange occupied the bulk of my waking hours. The pleasant bulk, anyway. It made no sense. I *knew* it didn't. But somehow, FONY had sunk her virtual claws into me. I started thinking about her in class, at lunch . . . I even broke my private rule and stared at a hundred different freshman girls in the halls, wondering and wondering: *Could it be . . . ?*

At the end of every school day, I raced home. I went through the day's e-mails on Naomi's computer until I found hers.

Incidentally, Naomi hadn't bothered to ask Mom and Aunt Ruth about hooking me up with Internet access. No big surprise there. But it didn't cause any conflict. Naomi was spending less and less time at home and more time with you-know-who. She was out almost every night of the week. And that gave me plenty of time to swap at least a dozen ludicrous e-mails with FONY before Naomi got back—at which point I would hastily find somebody with a real problem and dash off a response for the next day's column.

This isn't to say that I stopped caring about the column completely. I did care. But if anything, my obsession with FONY helped me deal with it, because if I cared *too* much—if I really thought about what was going on—I'd probably have a panic attack.

"Tell It to Naomi!" wasn't just popular anymore; it was a *sensation*.

It was petrifying.

For example:

A) A bunch of kids—clearly kids with too much time on their hands, like me—had posted an ad in the school paper for a new Web site to discuss what was being discussed in the column. *To give advice about my advice.*

B) I was already being spoofed, *Mad Magazine* style. Some wiseass had left a stack of anonymous cartoons in the cafeteria featuring a crude drawing of a girl sobbing into a horse's butt. Printed at the top were the words: TELL IT TO THE PONY!

C) Joel Newbury had told my sister that the faculty was taking bets about Naomi's real identity. The teachers' lounge pool was already up to six hundred dollars. (Among their theories, or at least the most troubling: I was Joel's mom.)

So Naomi was right; I was famous. Or *she* was. Or whatever. And as much as it pained me to admit it, Joel Horn-Rimmed was right about something, too: The column was definitely getting people to read the school paper again. *Definitely*.

I received at least a hundred e-mails a day. I'll never understand why. It couldn't have had anything to do with the quality of my slap-dash advice—although it might have helped that I'd given up on my anti-schmuck mission. (The mission officially died the night I caught Naomi humming to herself.) I chalked it up to boredom, pure and simple. And voyeurism. I figured the column's success was driven by the same kind of instinct that compels people to watch reality TV. For God's sake, *kids from other schools were writing in*. It was the Celeste Fanucci "I'm No Expert" Phenomenon, part deux. Take the Bad Kid, for example. She couldn't have gone to Roosevelt. It was a cruel school, to be sure, but there was no talk of making us wear uniforms. That I knew for certain.

I almost felt like enlisting Naomi to ask Celeste how she'd dealt with *her* success.

Almost.

I didn't want to have *any* sort of conversation with Celeste, though, not even through my sister. I could barely bring myself to say hi to her in the halls. I was over her. No, that isn't accurate enough: *I wanted nothing to do with her*—not since Zeke Beck had worked his hippie magic on her with his show at the Spiral Lounge . . . because after that, Celeste had made the final plunge into Ditz World. (She'd never bothered to write that article, either.) She and Zeke were most certainly an item now. They were one of those awful, giggly, let's-hug-in-public items.

She made me cringe. She made me want to puke. *She* was a schmuck. And remarkably, it didn't even bother me.

I didn't need Celeste Fanucci's help. I didn't even need my sister's help. I could handle the entire "Tell It to Naomi!" operation on my own. I had a system: Talk to FONY for five hours; write the column for someone else in five minutes. Ba-da-bing, ba-da-boom. It was easy. And for what got printed, I stuck mostly with the kids I'd known from the beginning, like S.O.M.B. I advised her to put her foot down. Her boyfriend *had* to start showering and brushing his teeth. He had to respect her.

Occasionally I'd even keep in touch with Hospital Girl. Not that I ever used *those* e-mails for the column. No . . . I still couldn't make up my mind whether she actually existed. So I refused to discuss her father. If she *was* playing a joke, I wouldn't go that far. Instead, I tutored her in the subtler nuances of the word G. (Example: "Whaddup, G!" as opposed to "Not cool, G.") I basically made fun of her "slangs." I told her that if she liked *Yo! MTV Raps,* she should also purchase Vanilla Ice's seminal *To the Extreme.* It was a true classic. Word to your mother.

Real or not, she seemed grateful. Or at least she pretended not to catch on that I was ragging on her. She wrote that she hated talking about her father. It only made her sadder. (At least, that's what I think she wrote.) She loved chatting with me because it took her mind off *him.* She wrote that she loved to chat about "THINGS NOT UGLY THAT IS TO SAY I SHOULD LIKE TO TALK ABOUT DR. SEUSS AND VANILLA ICE ICE BABY!"

And I was happy to oblige her.

Yes, even with a potential fraud like Hospital Girl, I channeled the chick inside me.

I know that sounds deranged. But it kept *my* mind off a certain ugly thing: namely, that I was still a loser. Or it did—until I started seeing pumpkins in every apartment window and cheap plastic skeletons in every bodega. Because that was when another ugly thing hit me.

Halloween is right around the corner.

Which meant that Cheese's birthday was right around the corner, too.

"Hey, look who it is! Dave Rosen!"

I'd just rushed home from school Wednesday—the last Wednesday in October—when I nearly slammed into Cheese's father on the stairwell, coming the other way.

It was about four o'clock. Normally I would have stopped to make some polite chitchat. But I knew there would be a FONY e-mail waiting for me upstairs. My feet kept moving.

"Oh, hey, Mr. Harrison," I said with a laugh. "How's it—"

I froze.

Cheese was lurking in the shadows behind him.

"We're just on our way out to pick up supplies," Mr. Harrison said. "You in the mood for anything special?"

My eyes narrowed.

I didn't get it. Mr. Harrison wasn't the kind of guy who ran errands for people, especially not me. He was the kind of guy who yelled at people. Me included.

"Uh . . . no thanks," I said uncertainly. "I'm fine."

Mr. Harrison smirked. "I wasn't offering to pick up a pizza for you, Dave. I meant for the party. You know, Saturday?"

The party?

I felt a strange tightness in my chest.

I stole a quick glance at Cheese. As usual, his hair covered his face. His gaze was fixed squarely on his Doc Martens.

I shook my head.

"Well, I know you like Sour Patch Kids," Mr. Harrison said, continuing down the steps. "I'll grab a bag. How's that sound?"

I nodded. My heart pounded.

I stared at Cheese as he shuffled right by me. He didn't say a word.

"Oh, and tell your family that they're invited, too, of course," Mr. Harrison added. He chuckled. "It'll take some of the pressure off them. For once, somebody *else* in the building will be blasting loud music. . . ."

He and Cheese rounded the corner to the lobby.

"See you Saturday night!" he called. "Nine p.m. sharp! Get ready to boogie. . . ."

The building door slammed behind them

I stood there on the stairs, my eyes wide.

I could barely breathe.

My God.

I'd always thought . . . I mean, I'd never imagined . . . There was just no way Cheese could ever celebrate his sixteenth birthday without me. It was the most important birthday of his *life*. He could start driving now. He was one year away from not having to sneak into NC-17 movies. The situation had gotten *that* out of control.

It's my fault, isn't it?

Of course it was. There was no denying it. Dealing with problems had never been Cheese's specialty. Not even as a kid. Instead of wiping his nose, he'd rather just twirl in circles. It had been up to me to fix things all along. *I* was the one who should have called every night until we'd hashed this out. *I* should have gone down there and pounded on his door until he'd answered. But after I'd tried that first time, I'd been too embarrassed—

Enough. There was no need to turn this into a calamity. Screw that. Relationships went through ups and downs. I'd seen enough e-mails to know *that*.

If Cheese wanted to ring in sweet sixteen without me, that was his prerogative. He had his own friends now, just as I had mine.

Right. What was I even thinking?

I turned and sprinted up to the fourth floor, taking three steps at a time.

* * *

You have 104 new messages

Time: 9:11 am
Subject: hello??? anybody home???

```
Time: 9:12 am
Subject: there's a dog on the next block whose spitty
Time: 9:13 am
Subject: this is the 8th e-mail I've sent you. how come
        you don't answer . . .
Time: 9:14 am
Subject: eating, drinking, smoking, failing
Time: 9:14 am
Subject: i'm scared of my shrink and i think i'm in love
        with you
Time: 9:16 am
Subject: those butterflies you get when you pee in the
        library
Time: 9:20 am
Subject: your column sucks so bad
Time: 9:21 am
Subject: this is the 9th email I've sent you.
Time: 9:22 am
Subject: (No Subject)
Time: 9:28 am
Subject: FONY needs help this time
```

(to view messages 11–20, click here)

My eyes zeroed right in on FONY. I was barely able to sit—in large part because I was still wearing my book bag. It hadn't even occurred to me to take it off.

I might as well have been *panting* over her e-mail.

Thank God FONY couldn't see this. In that instant I understood what a crack addict must feel like when he's about to light up. I was *that* hooked on her. (I know; I know . . . again with the crack. They really shouldn't make us watch those videos at school. They get to you. Let's say I felt like one of those fat guys on the wall of Don Vito's right before he's about to take a big bite of veal parmigiana.)

I perched on the edge of Naomi's chair—ignoring the algebra textbook digging into my spine—and clicked on the e-mail.

Dear Naomi,

This time you're really going to think I've lost it. I have to warn you up front: for once this has nothing to do with dreams, or with New York City and my irrational/natural fear/love thereof.

It has to do with a question I asked you a long time ago. Remember when . . . ?

Sorry. I'll stop procrastinating.

I have this boyfriend. I know this may seem surprising to you, seeing as a) I never mentioned him, b) I'm a total nutcase, and c) I don't really have any other friends besides him. Anyway, he's nice and smart and . . . okay. Can I be frank? He's HOT! He's smoking! ☺

See, that's what I really like about him. Sounds sick, I know. Bet you never knew how shallow I was. (Or did you?) Maybe that's why I've never mentioned him. I'm not sure how serious I can be about him. He doesn't have the greatest sense of humor. This is a BIG PROBLEM.

I also think he might be cheating on me.

Oh, yeah. That.☹

So Naomi . . . any advice for your old pal FONY?

I reread it. Then I clicked on the mouse again, exiting the program. Naomi's computer went blank.

Interesting, I thought. *FONY has a boyfriend.*

I tried to settle back in Naomi's chair. I couldn't, because of the book bag. So I did what any professional advice columnist would do: I removed my book bag and hurled it against Naomi's wall in a single, violent, deft maneuver: *smack!*

The floor shook.

Now . . . did I have any advice for my old pal FONY?

Yes. Yes, in fact, I did.

It was fourfold:

Dump cheating boyfriend; meet Dave Rosen; fall in love with Dave Rosen; marry Dave Rosen.

But how to word it . . .

Oh, right. I couldn't. I was Naomi. The chick. FONY's online gal pal.

Hmm. This was difficult. This was not the kind of e-mail from FONY I'd been hoping for. I'd been hoping for something along the lines of another new five-letter word for diarrhea. But I was not going to get upset. No. That would be unprofessional. And at such a pivotal moment a professional advice columnist like me starts to realize something very very important . . .

A girl you've never met before *could* be hideously ugly.

Right? She could have a beard of zits. She could have fat thighs. She could even look like Aunt Ruth's friend Joan—a woman who from certain angles resembled a tortoise. So the solution was ready-made. I had to find out what FONY looked like. Immediately. And in order to do so, I would have to trick her somehow. . . .

I let out a deep breath.

What was I worried about? There was no problem here. I'd already had plenty of experience tricking FONY.

It was all I'd ever done.

Chapter Seventeen

The old adage is true: nothing is ever as easy as it seems.

I tried to trick FONY three separate times over the next two days before I finally had sense enough to give up. If nothing else, I can say this: I stuck to the A-B-C format. I tried three times, and three times only. I think FONY would have appreciated that.

A) THE TIME I OFFERED TO JUDGE HER BOYFRIEND

This was in direct response to her e-mail. I wrote to her: a bad sense of humor was a big problem. The biggest. Only if her boyfriend was drop-dead gorgeous—an ancient Greek statue come to life—could she have an excuse for staying with him. So? I had to see him for myself. As a mentor and an older woman, I alone could make such a judgment on beauty. I suggested that we arrange a secret viewing; I had to remain anonymous. But if she could pick a street corner and plan to be there some time that afternoon with her boyfriend, I would sneak past and take a peek. What a crazy idea! she wrote. How about on Broadway right across from City Hall? In half an hour? Yes! I replied. I hopped on the subway, full of anticipation. There was a burst of static from the loudspeaker. The train was being rerouted. Next stop, DeKalb Avenue. The doors closed. I couldn't escape. The train sailed out high above the East River, lurching to a mysterious halt on the bridge, where it stayed for an hour. I watched the sunset over sparkles and skyscrapers and boats. Somewhere down below, FONY and her Adonis waited for me, then left. Later, when the train arrived in Brooklyn, the voice on the loudspeaker apologized "for the inconvenience."

B) THE TIME I SAID I WANTED TO GET MY BELLY BUTTON PIERCED, TOO

I was positive this would be a slam dunk. FONY still wanted a belly-button pierce, but she couldn't muster the courage to defy her conservative father. So I wrote to her: I had the same problem with my lunatic mother! I'd been thinking about a belly-button pierce for years now! We both just needed allies. Thursday, I suggested we make back-to-back appointments at the House of Body Art on 8th Street—a piercing/tattoo parlor and infamous haunt of some of the city's most frightening derelicts. Once again, we wouldn't meet in person. The plan? I would get pierced first and leave a photo of my belly with the proprietors, "proving" I'd done it. (In reality, of course, I'd just hide nearby until she showed, then run away once I'd identified her.) Agreed? What a crazy idea! she wrote. Will the piercing hurt? By the way, what did I think of her boyfriend? I never got a good look at him, I replied. (The truth.) Unfortunately, when I went to 8th Street a few hours later, I found it completely blocked off by fire engines and police cars. All that remained of the House of Body Art was a charred hole in the ground. A cop in a surgical mask told me that some homemade tattoo ink had exploded on the premises, and unless I wanted to breathe a "lungful o' toxic I-dunno-what," I should evacuate the area immediately.

C) THE TIME I TOLD HER TO GO TO OPEN-MIKE NIGHT

Strange forces seemed to be conspiring against me, so Friday I decided to play it safe. I doubted there would be a tattoo ink explosion at the Spiral Lounge. These sorts of catastrophes never occur two days in a row. Plus, the Spiral Lounge was within walking distance of my house. There was no danger of getting trapped on the subway. I wrote to FONY: she should give her boyfriend one final test on the humor front. She should take him to open-mike night! If he laughed at the silly fools who actually got up there and performed, then his sense of humor was fine! (Also, if she caught him checking out other chicks, she'd know he was a cheater.) Oddly, I never heard back from her. I decided to go the Spiral Lounge anyway. I spotted Zeke Beck half a block away, sitting on a stoop with some tall Asian girl. Zeke was caressing his guitar case. The girl was caressing Zeke. Strange, I thought. Maybe he and Celeste had broken up. Or maybe they were into free love. Whatever. I didn't care. What I did care about was the horrifying possibility of having to sit through Zeke's music. Still, the chance to identify FONY outweighed all other considerations. Or so I believed . . . until I saw Olga Romanoff laughing with her crew in line outside the club. "Hello? Is tonight not the perfect night for me to unveil my 'Naomi' stand-up routine? I mean, come on. You guys have read David Sedaris."

At that point, I called it quits and fled.

* * *

When I slunk back home, Mom and Aunt Ruth were waiting up for me. It wasn't late, maybe nine-thirty, but I could tell they were upset. They sat face to face in their pajamas at the kitchen table, hunched over mugs of decaf. James Brown hummed quietly from the stereo.

"Where have you been?" they demanded simultaneously.

I sighed. "You guys. I *told* you. I went to that open-mike thing."

"Don't 'you guys' me," Aunt Ruth said sternly. "We have a rule, Dave. Remember—"

"Ruth, please, I'll handle this," Mom interrupted. She looked me in the eye. "We have a rule, Dave. Remember?"

"What?" I said defensively. "Before I went to school this morning, I told you I might go to the Spiral Lounge tonight. Remember that?"

Mom shook her head. "You mentioned it in passing. You said you might go. And you never gave any indication about how late you would be. You didn't call or leave us a note. We had no idea where you were. What concerns me even more is that you went alone—"

"All right, all right," I muttered. "I'm sorry. Jeez."

"Dave, you have to leave a note or borrow Naomi's cell phone when you're out this late," Mom stated. "You could learn a thing or two from your sister. Naomi always calls or leaves a note when she's going to be out. Particularly if she's going out alone."

I laughed. "How can I borrow Naomi's cell phone? She's never home long enough for me to say hi to her."

"She's home right now," Aunt Ruth said. She sipped her decaf, eyebrows raised.

"She is?" I asked, genuinely shocked. "Why?"

"She lives here, Dave," Mom said dryly.

"Could've fooled me." I turned and hurried down the hall. If she *was* here, at the very least I knew she could shield me from the wrath of the Dueling Pajamas.

"Dave?" Mom called. "This conversation isn't over!"

"Let him go," Aunt Ruth moaned. "He can't escape now."

Indeed, Naomi was sitting on her unmade bed. The downside: she wasn't alone. *He* was sitting right next to her. Make that practically on top of her. I stood in her doorway fighting off the instinct to gag. I'd always hoped that some of Naomi's influence would change Joel Newbury for the better, that the shaved-and-black-leather look was just a tiny step (albeit an off-kilter step) toward self-improvement.

But he'd regressed. He'd gone back to the air tie.

A bald head, a leather jacket, and an air tie. God help us all.

Naomi kept jabbing at him, trying to unbutton the top button—but he kept squirming away, holding her arms back.

They both giggled hysterically. They didn't even notice I was there.

"Why do you *do* it?" she squealed.

"Because I *like* it."

"But it looks so stupid."

She lunged at his throat again. He spun away.

"Stupid as compared to what?" he asked. "Your hair? What's the problem with buttoning up my shirt? It's getting cold out. Your hair looks like that tattoo parlor that exploded on Eighth Street."

Naomi burst out laughing—then froze.

"Oh, hi, Dave!" she exclaimed. Her cheeks reddened. She pulled her hands back to her lap and slid away from him.

"Hey, Dave!" Joel cried. You'd think we were lifelong buddies.

Hey, dork! I answered silently.

"Speak of the devil," he said. "We were just talking about you."

I nodded. I didn't want to risk speaking. There was no way in hell I would call him Mr. Newbury. Not when he was in *my* house.

"Naomi says you've been helping her out with the column," he said. "She said if it wasn't for you, she wouldn't be able to do such a good job."

"She *said* that?" I asked.

Naomi grinned at me.

I almost grinned back. It was pure poker. She was daring me to break down and tell Joel the truth because she knew I wouldn't. (Not that he would have believed me, anyway.) But she was good, my sister. She was brilliant. She could a) control me, b) make her lame boyfriend feel like part of the family, and c) tell a convincing lie—all without even having to open her mouth.

"She says you have a knack for picking good subjects," he said.

"And that you're a great writer!" Naomi added.

I pursed my lips. Now she was trying to appease me for keeping our secret. *Jerk.* Unfortunately, it worked.

"Anyway," Joel continued, "I've been thinking, and I might have a spot for you in my creative writing class. It's a yearlong course, and I generally prefer to give it to juniors and seniors. But Naomi has been talking you up so much . . . well, I have to do something to shut her up." He laughed. "No, it's not that. I trust her opinion."

They exchanged smiles.

For a horrifying second, I thought they might kiss.

"I'm gonna go to my room," I said.

"Wait!" Joel said. "Does this sound like something that interests you?"

I shrugged. "Sure."

"A student just dropped out of the class today, so I have a space available," he said. He shook his head, as if remembering a private joke. "And believe me, I have *no* doubt that your writing will be far superior to hers."

"Naomi says I'm that good, huh?" I asked sarcastically.

Joel chuckled. "Well, it's not so much that. No offense. It's just . . . English isn't this student's first language. In fact, I'm not even sure *what* her first language is. She claims she's from France, but her French is pretty poor, too."

I stared at him.

"She's from France?" I asked.

"That's what *she* said," Joel said. "We only talked once, if you can call it that. She never raised her hand or participated in class. After our little conversation I understood why. Her speech . . ." He didn't finish.

I felt an unpleasant tingle. "What do you mean, her speech?"

"Well I could barely comprehend a word of hers—in French *or* in English," he said. "I don't know how she's gotten by so far. In fact, I think she might be leaving Roosevelt. That was the impression I got."

"Where . . . where in France is she from?" I stammered.

"A small town. In the south."

"Which one?"

"Pau, I believe," he said.

A black dizziness swept over me. "Pau," I echoed.

"Yes." He laughed, puzzled. "Why? Do you know it?"

"Yeah . . . I mean, no," I croaked. My mouth was suddenly dry. I clutched at the doorframe. "Uh . . . where—um, what's her name?"

Joel frowned. "Hafida Something. I think it's Arabic. Why? What's—"

"Hey, Dave, are you all right?" Naomi interrupted. "You look sort of pale."

"I . . . um, I'm just tired." My voice quavered. "Can—uh, can I ask you something else, Jo—Mr. Newbury? Why . . . why do you think she's leaving school?"

"I have no idea," he said. He shot Naomi a concerned look, then glanced back at me. "Do you know this student, Dave?"

"I . . . " *Crap.* I should have kept my mouth shut. I couldn't lie now; I was in too deep. They *knew* I knew her. It was obvious. Any excuse would sound like BS. "I just thought I recognized her from when I was helping Naomi with the column," I said. "I think one of the girls who wrote in mentioned that she'd lived in France. I thought she might make a good subject. You know, since she's from a different country. I thought she could give people a different perspective on things. That's all."

Joel stared at me.

My breathing quickened.

Naomi stared at me, too. Her face was blank. I had no idea what she was thinking.

"I see," Joel said. He turned to my sister. "Did you ever see anything from a girl from France?" he asked.

She chewed her lip. "No. Not that I remember."

Amazing, I thought bitterly—although the bitterness was directed as much at myself as it was at my sister. For once, Naomi was telling the God's honest truth, and for once, she sounded like she was lying. She'd never seen anything from Hospital Girl. Why would she have? I'd never used Hospital Girl for our stupid column. I'd kept her to myself. I'd dealt with her all on my own, time after time, never quite believing she'd existed. Playing along with her as a joke, trying to see if she would break down, because her ridiculous syntax entertained me . . .

"Dave, let me ask you a question," Joel said. "Do you think this girl is in some kind of trouble? I mean, I don't mean to pry. But is there something you want to tell us?"

Uh-oh. If I'd been looking for an exit cue, I'd definitely found it.

"I'm just tired," I said. "I've had a lousy night. It's nothing. Believe me. Really, I'd tell you if it was anything. Good night, you guys."

Before they could say another word, I bolted to my room and locked the door.

Chapter Eighteen

Aunt Ruth was wrong.

I *could* escape.

True, I hadn't snuck out in over a year—not since the summer before last, when Cheese and I had clandestinely attended a midnight showing of *This Is Spinal Tap* at the Film Forum. I'd grown a little since then, too. Or rather, I'd aged. This may not seem like an important distinction, but it was. It was a point of pride, really. Cheese and I had always maintained that only two types of people could squirm through the narrow window in my bedroom: prepubescent boys and female yoga instructors.

As a *man,* I would be screwed.

But on that night—big surprise—manhood was still a long way off. I slithered onto the fire escape with the agility of a snake. (*Snake* in this case meaning "prepubescent boy" or "female yoga instructor.")

As quietly as I could, I closed the window behind me. *Damn.* It was pretty cold out. I climbed down the steep metal ladders, hand over hand—the metal rungs felt like ice—and swung down, jungle gym style, into the alley behind our building. My knees buckled. I shivered. I probably should have worn a jacket . . . but nah.

I didn't have far to go.

* * *

"Yes, dear? May I help you?"

If you're ever looking to feel *truly* unmanly, try having an old-woman security guard call you "dear." Luckily, I was too distracted to pay much attention. I felt kind of bad for her. I wouldn't want to work the desk at St. Vincent's at midnight on a Friday, especially not in that beige polyester rent-a-cop uniform. She should have been home in bed. She looked a good ten years older than Mom and Aunt Ruth, at least. She wore bifocals.

"Um . . . yes," I said. My lungs heaved. I was still out of breath from the ten-block run to the hospital. "Thank you. I'm looking for a patient. . . ." I glanced around the waiting room. It was packed with the sorriest, most miserable-looking crowd I'd ever seen. *So this is what they mean when they talk about "your huddled masses,"* I thought with creeping depression.

"What's the name?" she asked.

I turned back to her and tried to smile. "Um . . . I'm not sure."

"Excuse me?"

"See, I don't know the name. I know that he's an Algerian with some kind of liver disease. He's an alcoholic. He . . . oh, yeah—he was nearly kicked out of here for sexually harassing a nurse." My face brightened. "That should narrow it down, right?"

The woman squinted at me through her glasses.

"Is there a problem?" I asked.

"Let me get this straight, young man," she replied in a flat voice. "You're looking for an alcoholic who harasses nurses. And you don't know his name."

I swallowed. "Yeah, but I know his daughter's name. It's Hafida. She's the one I really want to see, actually. I know she spends weekends with him—"

"Save it," the woman interrupted. "You got a picture ID?"

"Yeah . . ." I jammed my fist into my pocket and pulled out my school card. It was draped in old Sour Patch Kid wrappers and a torn five-dollar bill. (One of these days I would have to get a wallet.) I cleaned off the debris and handed it to her.

She frowned, but took it. "David Rosen," she murmured, examining the card. "Roosevelt High."

"Yup. That's me."

"All right." She fixed me with a hard stare. "I'm gonna hold on to this. I'm also gonna let the security guard up on six know that you're coming. So if there's any monkey business, you'll be in big trouble."

I shook my head. "No monkey business. I swear."

She smiled, satisfied. "Okay, then. The sixth floor is where you want to go. Take the elevator at the end of the hall. Somebody there can help you."

"Thanks." I turned to run.

"Wait!" she barked. "You have to sign in." She shoved a big open book across the desk.

"Oh . . . okay." I grabbed the pen and started scrawling my name underneath a list of about two dozen other signatures.

All at once, my arm seized up.

At the top of the page, a name leaped out and bored into my eyeballs.

HAFIDA AL-SAIF

Written in all caps.

"Is there a problem?" the security guard asked.

"No, none at all," I choked out. "Thank you."

I dropped the pen and sprinted into the waiting elevator. My head spun. A fuzzy *whoosh* filled my ears; I couldn't hear anything except the pounding of my own blood. I jabbed at the sixth-floor button. The elevator slowly ascended—slowly, slowly . . . as slowly as the train that had gotten stuck on the bridge to DeKalb Avenue. I paced back and forth.

Ding!

The doors parted.

I dashed out, skidding to a halt by the nurses' station. Nearby, an old security guard—a man—chatted with several interns in green scrubs.

They glanced at me.

Where, where, where—
There.

My legs turned to jelly.

Curled up on a couch in the little waiting area, right next to the coffee machine, was a girl I recognized from Roosevelt. She was skinny, very dark-skinned, with long dreadlocks. She was listening to a bulky yellow Walkman. It was the old-fashioned kind, for cassettes. The Walkman was the only reason I'd noticed her at school in the first place. Nobody listens to cassettes.

I'd never said a single word to her.

I'd never heard her *say* a single word, either. She was a Clark Kent, like me. The few times I'd seen her, she was always alone—wearing her Walkman, lost in music.

I couldn't move. I could only stand there, staring. She was less than twenty feet away.

Hospital Girl.

Who else could it be? Was some other girl from Roosevelt hanging out in the exact same ward as Hafida Al-Saif at midnight on a Friday? What were the odds of that?

Then I asked myself something else.

What the hell am I even doing here?

Now, *that* was a good question. I didn't have a clue. I hadn't had a single coherent thought since I'd slammed the door on Naomi and Joel. I guess I must have acted on a deranged compulsion to prove that Hospital Girl did exist, or that she didn't . . . or that I was the biggest schmuck on the planet for having treated her like a joke all this time. But it wasn't as if I'd had a *plan*. What was I supposed to do? Walk right up to her and say: "Hi, are you Hospital Girl? Because I'm Naomi, and I just thought I'd pop in for a visit? And Vanilla Ice actually sucks? And I thought you might like to know that I'm really a fifteen-year-old boy?"

Suddenly I realized she was looking right at me.

She smiled shyly, then sat up straight and took off her headphones. *Oh, God.* She must have recognized me from school, too. . . .

I panicked.

She waved.

No, no, no. I whirled and jabbed my finger into the elevator call button. The doors opened right away. I jumped inside—cramming myself into a corner to hide from her—and started maniacally swatting at the first-floor button.

I couldn't hide from the security guard, though. He stood there with the interns, watching. He didn't seem too happy with me.

I almost wanted to tell him that I was on his side. I wasn't too happy with me, either.

* * *

After that . . . I guess I must have walked for a long time. I eventually ended up down by Ground Zero, which is about thirty blocks south of St. Vincent's. The memory of the trip is pretty cloudy, though. Trying to describe it would be like trying to describe a faded dream or the plot of a movie at the Three-Dollar Theater.

I just *walked,* with no thought other than putting as much distance as possible between Hospital Girl and me.

I do remember that the streets seemed warmer, though. It might have had something to do with my overactive, overstressed circulation. But I think it was also because the city was so crowded, even well after midnight. It had become a big, swirling hive of bodies—mostly kids Naomi's age, in couples, in posses—and all of them buzzing, buzzing: hailing cabs, laughing, scheming . . . pretty much looking for the next big event. Cheese used to call it night feeding.

The whole scene reminded me of the last time I'd snuck out with him, in fact. Neither of us could believe how many people came alive so late at night. Especially when *This Is Spinal Tap* was over. That audience . . . Man, they were the *real* night feeders. Cheese kept eavesdropping on people's conversations as we hurried out of the theater. "Did you hear that?" he would whisper, grinning in wide-eyed ecstasy. It was clear to him: we'd hit the sneak-out mother lode. Everybody was talking about some bar or party they were going to hit.

153

"We gotta pick a crew and tag along with them," he whispered once we were outside.

I laughed. "I don't know, man."

"What's not to know?" His eyes flashed over the crowd. "Come on, Dave. We're already out on the town. We're *committed*. When do your mom and aunt wake up? Not until seven at least, right? That gives us five whole hours."

"Yeah, but . . ." I stifled a yawn. "I'm pretty beat."

"You just need a second wind. Picture it, Dave. You and me. We're kicking it at some illegal after-hours gambling joint. We both have fine honeys on our arms. Two. Meaning two *apiece*. And the owners are getting pissed. We got their ladies; we got their loot . . . and there's gonna be some drama because we've taken them for all their cash! But we're *ready*, man! You know! And—"

"Cheese?"

"Yeah?" he said, unable to contain himself.

"Do you really think that's gonna happen?"

"I'm sure something *better* will happen," he said.

I laughed again. "Whatever. I'm going to sleep."

"Really?"

"Yeah, really," I moaned. I walked to the curb and raised my arm to hail a cab.

He shook his head. "I think we're blowing something here." He gazed in longing as the last of the *Spinal Tap* night feeders melted into the darkness. "I really think we're blowing it. . . ."

"Blowing what?"

A cab screeched up beside me.

Cheese sighed. "That's the whole point, Dave. We'll never know now. Will we?"

Chapter Nineteen

It wasn't until I started shivering again that I noticed how far I'd walked. The floodlights over Ground Zero towered above me, maybe five or six blocks away. They were brighter than the lights at Yankee Stadium. I'd never been this close. Mom and Aunt Ruth refused to go. So did Naomi.

I wanted to see it, though. Eventually. Needless to say, however, taking a solitary tour of Ground Zero at that particular moment didn't seem like the greatest idea.

But it occurred to me . . . if I was this far downtown, I was also near another, very different landmark: City Hall. I almost chuckled.

Too bad I hadn't arranged for FONY to show me her boyfriend tonight. Everything would have worked out perfectly.

Ha!

Yes, truly, life *can* be a real crack-up sometimes.

I glanced up at the street signs. I was at West Broadway and Duane Street (facing a two-mile, two-subway trip back to my bedroom), and it was cold. It was also nearly two in the morning. My feet ached, too. Even the night feeders had begun to thin out.

But I knew that if I went back home, I'd just lie awake in bed. I'd stare at the ceiling and obsess about what a jerk I'd been to Hospital Girl. Or . . . had I been a jerk? I wasn't even sure. *She* was the one who hadn't wanted to talk about her father. And if I'd really been *that* big of a jerk, she wouldn't have kept writing in—

That's when I noticed it.

A neon sign: COPY CORNER. It was just down the block, on the other side of the intersection—one of those twenty-four-hour Xerox/fax/Internet-access places.

Hmm.

I still had the torn five on me. The glass windows were brightly lit. It looked warm in there. I could send Hospital Girl an e-mail right now. . . .

I ran toward the door.

As is often the case when I'm up much later than normal, my mind wasn't exactly clear. I shoved the bill at the guy behind the counter and took a seat at an empty computer terminal. Surprisingly, the place was pretty crowded, probably with tortured loners and losers like me. Not that I got a good look at any of them. No, I was in too much of a hurry to figure out exactly *how* I could tell Hospital Girl that I was sorry for ragging on her—without appearing *too* sorry, because I didn't want to give myself away. . . .

I clicked on to the "Tell It to Naomi!" server.

I couldn't believe it. Or, no, I *could*.

I should have known. . . .

I should have gone to bed.

There was only one e-mail waiting for me:

Time: 11:43 pm
Subject: FONY and Naomi have to talk

My fingers moistened as I opened it.

Dear Naomi,

Where to begin? I KNOW the A-B-C format won't work in this case. I don't mean to sound so serious, like I'm

mad at you. Actually, the OPPOSITE is true. Okay . . .
I'm rambling, and procrastinating has never been my
specialty . . . I'll get right to it.

I'm going out on a limb:

Is it my imagination, or do you want to meet me in
person?

I guess what I'm really asking is: are we friends?
Like not just advice colum-NIST and colum-NEE, but
real friends? Because I feel like we are. Maybe it's
just because your e-mails have changed so much over
the past couple of days. You never used to come up
with crazy ideas to DO things together. Or as close
as you can get to doing things together without
breaking the advice columnist wall . . . and it's not
that I mind . . . God . . . hardly . . . I'm SO
PYSCHED! I've been WAITING FOR THIS!

I have a feeling I know who you are.

I have a feeling you're Naomi Rosen. (And if
you're not, please spare me the embarrassment.
Just tell me, and I swear I'll never write to you
again.)

But the reason I'm so sure I know is because we spoke
on the phone once, a long time ago. Before you even
started writing the column. (I also called you again
after that—did you ever get the message? Never
mind . . .) I know this sounds completely crazy, but
I felt like we made a connection on the phone that
day. And . . . oh, boy . . . this is going to sound

even MORE crazy. But I feel like, maybe, just maybe, you got the advice columnist idea from ME?

Is that possible? I'm sure I'm just patting myself on the back. I don't know if you even remember me. So here it goes . . . (I'm dying here . . .)

I'm Celeste Fanucci.

I actually know your little brother Dave from school. (He's so funny, btw!) But if I'm not going out on a limb, if you DO remember me . . . I just want to thank you. You really showed me how an advice column should be written. And the reason I never wanted to ask YOU for any advice is because I know how hard it can be as an advice columnist. I guess that was how we started exchanging e-mails about other stuff and becoming friends and . . .

Oh, God! Listen to me! This is so embarrassing! But I'm not going to censor myself. I'm just going to plug ahead and finish this e-mail and send it, for better or for worse. Because most of all I want to THANK YOU for making me see the light about my boyfriend. Because when you wrote that stuff about Spiral Lounge . . . see, the thing is, he PLAYS there. Every single open-mike night, he plays. He played tonight! And I just couldn't bring myself to go. It IS silly! HE'S silly! And he got all mad at me, like: Oh, what? You have to sit at your computer all night, like you always do? Talking to your "friend"? Rather than see me play?

He's JEALOUS of you! Can you believe that?

Maybe I should have seen him play. Maybe I should
break up with him. I don't even know. Because he is
sweet, if a bad musician and a little lacking on the
humor front. And he IS hot . . . hee, hee . . .

Okay, now I'll stop.

Again—if you aren't Naomi Rosen, you don't have to
respond. But if you are . . .
a) I'd like to meet in person, too. SO MUCH!
b) You RULE!!! I can't even tell you.
c) What should I do about Zeke!!??? (That's my
boyfriend. ☺)

—Celeste "FONY" Fanucci

The color had drained from my face.

I'd been turned into a sponge. Call it symbolism; call it anything
you want. But I *was* a sponge: a stupid, simple organism, the
simplest—existing in perfect ignorance, floating blindly through
wherever, not knowing squat about the real world . . . until the moment of death. (Death being the lone reality every organism under-
stands.) Because Celeste Fanucci, without ever laying a hand on me,
had ended my life. She'd wrung all the blood from my body. She'd
twisted and squeezed me, milking every last drop—

You get the picture.

This changed things.

I wasn't so upset about Hospital Girl anymore, for starters.
I turned away from the computer, catching a glimpse of my reflection
in one of the windows. I was white as a sheet. I just . . . *Okay*. I just
didn't understand how this was possible. FONY was a *freshman*.

She'd said so in her first e-mail—*the very first one she'd ever written.* Or she'd implied as much. And that wasn't my imagination. No. She'd *lied* to me. She'd *misled* me. If I'd known . . .

I laughed coldly.

No point in asking. *If I'd done X, then I would have known Y.* That was algebra. I didn't need algebra. I knew there was no variable in *this* equation.

I knew the truth.

What else did I know? I knew that I had *nothing* to say to this ditz who wasn't a ditz, this *actress* who pretended to believe in palm readings because she thought Zeke Beck was so freaking hot. And, plus— I knew that I wasn't Naomi Rosen. I was her funny little brother. So, technically, I didn't have to respond to the e-mail. But . . .

I couldn't just leave it at that. Celeste and I had a history together.

Our history.

Our history being (in condensed, Cliffs Notes form): I'd fallen in love with her; I'd sent her straight into the arms of a cheating scumbag with my brilliant advice; I'd fallen *out* of love with her; I'd fallen in love with someone else—someone smarter and funnier and *my type*—for once, a realistic possibility for me in the romance department, a freshman . . . and somehow I'd ended up right back where I'd started: in a lonely, lonely, lonely spongelike abyss.

Right. *That* history.

Still, regardless of all that, I owed Celeste a response. She wanted advice about how to deal with her boyfriend. And I was a published advice columnist—*her* published advice columnist.

But this wasn't the sort of advice I could give at two-thirty in the morning. I would have to sleep on this one.

I might even have to do some research.

Oh, yes. No doubt. I know just where to look, too.

She'd said I was funny? I'd *give* her funny.

There was only one suitable archive, one sick trove of blather (as in S-I-C-K)—*one source alone* that was vile, absurd, and altogether offensive enough to ensure that Celeste would never ask me for advice again.

And I'd never even read it.

But still, I was certain . . .

Grandpa Meyer's memoirs could set Celeste Fanucci straight.

Chapter Twenty

"This isn't like him at all," Aunt Ruth was whispering. "He never sleeps this late."

I blinked, rubbing my eyes. Sunlight was streaming through my windows.

What the—

Aunt Ruth was standing there with Cheese.

"Hey," I managed, wincing. "What's going on?"

"You tell me," Aunt Ruth muttered. She turned and headed toward the kitchen. "This isn't healthy, Dave. You've been in bed for fifteen hours. I really should talk to your mother. Your behavior recently . . ." Her voice faded into silence.

Cheese grinned at me.

"Really, Dave," he said, doing a dead-on impersonation of Aunt Ruth. "This isn't healthy at all."

I grinned back. For a beautiful, fleeting, disoriented moment, I'd been transported back into the past. All was well. Cheese was Cheese. He wasn't wearing a black suit jacket or Doc Martens—just jeans and his old homemade KISS ME, I'M LEGAL! T-shirt, and socks, because he'd obviously just run up the stairs from his apartment.

"Hey, man," I said.

"Hey, man, yourself." He closed the door and leaned against it. "What's going on? Are you sick are something?"

I shook my head. "No. Why?"

"It's two o'clock in the afternoon," he said. "You're passed out like a syllabus."

"Wow." I yawned. "I must have . . . I had a hard time falling asleep."

"Yeah, well look—I, uh, I just wanted to tell you that I'm canceling the party tonight."

"You're . . . what?"

He looked down at the floor. "I'm canceling the party tonight. Mike and Darren and I wanted to play at it—you know, acoustic—but Darren's sick. He can't make it. So we're gonna wait until next Saturday."

Now I was awake. He and his clones wanted to play "acoustic" tonight, huh? How nice. Too bad Darren was sick. Maybe Zeke Beck could fill in for him. Or at least provide Cheese with a tape loop. I almost suggested as much—but then I remembered, *Oh, right.* This had nothing to do with me. It was none of my business. I hadn't been invited to the party in the first place.

Cheese laughed to himself and looked up at me. "So . . . um, Dave? Is there anything you want to tell me?"

My face twisted in a scowl. That was the exact same question Joel Newbury had asked me last night. "What the hell is that supposed to mean?" I demanded hoarsely. "What would I want to tell *you?*"

His face darkened. He turned and reached for the doorknob. "Nothing. So—"

"You don't have to invite me to your party if you don't want to," I heard myself snap. I wished I hadn't, but there was nothing I could do about it now. It was out in the open. That dumb lump had found its way back into my throat, too.

"That wasn't what I was talking about," he mumbled, his back still turned.

"It wasn't? Well, please, *Greg.* Tell me. What are you talking about?"

He bowed his head. "Dave . . . I . . . forget it. I *wanted* to invite you to the party. That's what I'm doing right now. It's next Saturday. And your family's invited, too."

Before I could respond, he hurried out of the room.

I swallowed.

A moment later I heard the front door slam.

My eyes began to sting.

Nice, Dave, I thought. *Way to go. Free, again!*

Somehow, at some point, I'd developed a serious problem. I'd started handling every single situation exactly the way it *shouldn't* be handled. I needed a Rewind button for my life. A big, huge, cosmic Rewind button—for all sorts of things . . . to go back to the day Cheese asked to borrow my stupid guitar, for one. Why hadn't I just *let* him borrow it? Why had I picked this stupid fight in the first place? I never played my guitar. I hadn't picked it up in over a month. I hadn't *noticed* it, to be honest—or anything else I owned, really— not since I'd begun locking myself away in Naomi's room at all hours. . . .

Which reminded me.

I had work to do.

And I was just angry and demoralized enough to do it.

"Hey, Dave?" Mom yelled from the kitchen.

"Yeah?"

"Ruth and I are going out to shop for a DVD player. Do you want to come?"

"No thanks," I shouted back.

There was a pause.

"Oh, Dave, come on," Aunt Ruth pleaded. "We'll wait for you, okay? It's so nice out. We'll take you out for lunch. It's not good to be cooped up here so much—"

"I'm FINE!" I barked.

She didn't answer.

I could hear them muttering. *Oh, brother.* I threw the covers aside and tumbled out of bed, stomping across the room to poke my head out the door.

"I'm fine!" I repeated, peering down the hall. "Okay? Just go ahead!"

They stood huddled together in the kitchen, gaping at me. If I didn't know better, I'd say I'd just caught them in the middle of committing a crime. Or vice versa.

"You really don't want us to take you to lunch?" Aunt Ruth asked tentatively.

I forced a smile. "No. Thanks. It's just . . . I have work to do. That's all. Everything is fine. Really."

She opened her mouth again, but Mom grabbed her arm.

"We'll just go by ourselves, then, Ruth," she stated in a loud voice. She marched toward the front door, dragging Aunt Ruth along with her. "We'll be back by suppertime. Dave can stay here. If that's what he wants, that's what he gets. He's old enough to make these sorts of decisions for himself. He knows we'd love nothing better than for him to come with us, and to open up, and to share—to get whatever's troubling him so much off his chest—but we are not going to interfere with his decision-making. . . ."

The door closed behind them.

Whew.

I let out a deep breath.

Now: to dig up Grandpa Meyer's forbidden memoirs.

* * *

Mom's tiny bedroom is just around the corner from the bathroom. For some reason she has the smallest room in the apartment—even smaller than Aunt Ruth's. It was originally intended to be a study, I think, but since the four of us need privacy, we've always had to be a little creative with our living space.

I hurried down the hall. I was pretty sure she kept Grandpa Meyer's old chest in her shoe closet. Not that I'd ever seen it in there—or looked—but Naomi had once told me that Mom and Aunt Ruth hid all the family's embarrassing belongings in Mom's shoe closet. . . .

And as usual, when it came to secrets, Naomi was right.

The chest sat on the closet floor, smack in the middle of a bunch of boxes.

I grinned, kneeling down beside it. It looked exactly the same as I remembered it from the shivah at the retirement home—dust and all. The jimmied lock still hung open.

Carefully, with both hands, I raised the lid with and peered inside.

The pages were neatly stacked, if a little dirty. But they were still legible.

Rosen on Rosen:
The Life and Times of a Jewish American Romantic
By Meyer I. Rosen

I begin with a question. What is Love?

Ah . . . indeed. It is the oldest question.

Is Love merely a savage duet? Is Love the sweaty ballet that occurs between two people at their most intimate? Or perhaps more than two people, as is rumored to occur in some exotic countries, such as France? Can Love be defined by that uncontrollable moment when our tangled passions scream to be released, in wanton abandon, like a good sneeze?

Friends, I believe that Love is more profound than that.

For the mind does not exist apart from the body. Mind and body are one.

Consider Mrs. Slotnick—the pretty young woman across the street. At this very moment, as I write, looking through the blinds, I can see her frolicking in the nude. Is she remembering last night's romp with her husband? Is she listening to the radio? Is she just acting upon a wild animalistic instinct to dance?

Friends, I believe that the answers are more profound.

I closed the lid.

There was no need to read any further. No, I'd gotten the gist. I dashed out of the room, nearly tripping on the hall rug.

I understood something vital at that moment.

For the past seven years Mom and Aunt Ruth had hidden the memoirs from me, not because they were "inappropriate for children" (which, of course, they were), but for a more protective reason: Mom and Aunt Ruth had been trying to shield me from the knowledge that I was the direct descendant of a Peeping Tom.

I already knew that I had an irresponsible drunk on one side of the family. But now knowing for certain that I had a full-fledged pervert on the other? *Good God.* And what about all those people at the retirement home who used to say that Grandpa Meyer and I were "a lot alike"? How? How the hell was I like *him*?

I shuddered.

Sometimes it's best to follow the rules, I told myself as I hurried back around the corner. *Sometimes the rules are put in place for a reason. The next time I want to break a rule—no matter how dumb it may seem—I should remember what I just saw. . . .*

Right.

More to the point: consulting the memoirs was out. I would just have to trust my own instincts in responding to Celeste. But that was fine. My own instincts had always served me well when it came to the column. Just not when it came to anything else.

I burst into Naomi's room.

To my surprise, Naomi was sitting at the computer.

"Hey!" I said. "I didn't even know you were here."

"How could you know?" she said. "You've been asleep all day."

I frowned. "Why *are* you here, by the way?"

She kept her eyes fixed to the screen. "Dave, you do remember that this is my room, right? I know it can get confusing for you. I *am* extraordinarily generous with it."

I rolled my eyes and sat on her bed. "You didn't answer the question."

"Why am I here?" she said absently. "Why am I here . . . ?" She pecked at the keyboard. "I have work to do."

Interesting. That was exactly what I'd told Mom and Aunt Ruth. "You know what I don't get?" I grumbled. "It's fine for you to stay 'cooped up' all day, sleeping until all hours and sitting at the computer, but when *I* want to do that, it's suddenly cause for panic— Wait." I stared at her. "You said you had work to do?"

She nodded.

I felt the beginnings of a smile on my face. I wouldn't have thought it possible. "What kind of work? Did you get a job?" I asked.

"Well . . . yeah. I guess I did."

"Naomi, that's awesome! Congratulations—"

"Wait, wait." She spun around in the chair. "Thanks. I mean it. But look, don't say anything about it to Mom and Aunt Ruth, all right?"

"Why not?"

"It's . . . see, nothing's quite definite. It's all so up in the air right now." She smiled with a strange uncertainty.

"What is?"

Naomi leaned forward and lowered her voice. "Okay. Here's the deal. You know how I've been hanging out so much with Joel and his friend Brian?"

"No." My voice was a dull monotone. "You have? Really?"

"Dave," she groaned. "Can you can the humor? See, the two of them are putting together a business plan to launch a magazine. They've decided to start their own company. And they want me to be the magazine's centerpiece!"

Centerpiece?

My thoughts must have still been mired in "Rosen on Rosen" because for an awful moment . . . "What do you mean?" I asked, aghast. "They want you to pose for pictures? You don't need a job *that* bad—"

"Not center*fold*, you moron." She giggled. "Center*piece*. Jeez, Dave. You really have to get your mind out of the gutter. It's going to

168

be an educational magazine. Or maybe not so much educational as . . . well, it'll be sort of like the *New Yorker* for kids—but hipper, more cutting-edge, more fun. It was Brian's idea. He is, like, the hugest fan of the column. He thinks it's brilliant. But he thinks we should scrap the whole anonymity thing and go in the *opposite* direction. He thinks we should turn me into a *personality*. You know, like Dr. Ruth. He thinks the reason it's such a hit at school is because the kids who write in feel like they *know* me, like I'm their friend. And if they actually *did* know me—or, at least, if they knew who I was, if they could see my picture and learn about my life and stuff—then the column would *explode*. You know?"

She gazed at me expectantly.

I didn't answer.

I was a little annoyed.

As usual, Naomi sounded like a total madwoman. (I mean: "The *New Yorker* for kids"?) But I'd gotten used to her delusional monologues. That wasn't what bothered me. What bothered me was just one small detail . . . or rather, the *lack* of one small detail. In all her enthusiastic jabbering, she hadn't brought *me* up once. She'd never said "you, Dave." She'd said that the kids who wrote in felt like they knew *her*. Like *she* was their friend. That "the" column was brilliant—not *my* column; "the" column.

"So," she concluded, making up for my silence, "I'm here because I'm working on a little speech. Joel asked me to give it Monday afternoon."

"You're . . ." I shook my head. "A *speech*? What are you talking about?"

She laughed. I'd never seen her look more pleased with herself in her life.

"I've been waiting all morning to tell you this," she said. "Joel and Brian and I decided that I should reveal my identity. Joel is organizing a special assembly for after classes Monday. Anyone who's a fan of the column is welcome to come. He's going to announce it on the Web site and in the paper and at lunch." She couldn't keep still. The faster the words tumbled out of her mouth, the more she squirmed in her chair. "And Brian's going to be there, too. He's going to cover the whole thing for a special article in the *Voice*. He says that if the article makes enough of a splash, it'll get potential investors interested—and *that* will give us the money we need to get the magazine off the ground. You know what he said? He said he has a good shot at turning me into a local celebrity! A real-life Carrie Bradshaw, à la *Sex and the City*. Can you believe it?"

I sat still on her bed for a long moment. "Let me get this straight," I said.

"Yeah?"

"You're coming to my school on Monday. You're going to tell everybody that *you're* the real Naomi."

She nodded.

"And . . . that's it?"

"Well—yeah. I mean, no." She seemed confused. "This is just the first step. This is gonna change everything."

"Change everything," I repeated.

She nodded again.

For the first time I could remember—for the very first time in my *life*—Naomi wasn't tuning in to my tone of voice. This was disconcerting. Because I didn't just sound angry. I didn't just sound frustrated. I sounded *hostile*. And if she couldn't hear that, then drastic measures had to be taken.

I had to spell it out for her. Concisely.

I had to tell her that, in fact, *nothing* would change. *She* would be catapulted into the firmament of local celebrity. *I*, on the other hand, would continue to do all the work. I would continue to toil in solitude and obscurity, to answer the hundreds of e-mails from the hundreds of kids out there who were AT THE END OF THEIR ROPE and felt like SCREAMING. And since I fit neatly into both of those categories . . . since I'd just had my heart crushed like an insect by phony FONY; since my ex-best friend had invited me to his party only because his father had accidentally mentioned it; since I had nobody to talk to except—

"You've got mail!" Naomi's computer announced.

I clenched my fists at my sides.

Naomi laughed. "Oops!" she said. "I forgot to close the Internet window." She turned and clicked the mouse, squinting at the screen. "Hey, what do you know? One of my fans . . ."

"One of *your* fans," I said.

"Yeah. It says 'fat for Halloween.' . . . " She clicked the mouse again, her eyes zipping to the bottom of the e-mail. "Oh, yeah. It's from S.O.M.B. She's written in before, right?"

"Right," I heard myself say.

Naomi stood up.

I stood, too.

"Wanna reply?" Naomi asked, stretching. "You can sit in the hot seat for a while. I'm gonna grab some olives from the kitchen."

Unfortunately, the "hot seat" was a little *too* hot for me. It had burned me before. It had burned me just last night. The only reason I'd barged into Naomi's room today was to burn somebody *back*—to take out my rage and misery on Celeste, to sever all ties with her, and to make sure that she never wrote to me again.

But I'd learned my lesson.

I wouldn't risk getting burned again.

No, to quote a timeworn phrase: "Silence speaks louder than words." There was no need to respond to Celeste. She would get the picture. Come to think of it, *everybody* would get the picture— because if I sat in the "hot seat" one more time, my butt would surely be fried.

"You know what?" I said.

"What?" Naomi asked.

"*You* answer S.O.M.B."

Her smile faltered. "Me?"

"Yes. You. *You* deal with her problems. *You* offer her advice. *You* be the fake advice columnist for once, because I'm finished. I quit."

With that, I marched out and slammed the door in my sister's face.

Chapter Twenty-one

Half an hour later I heard Naomi's knock on my door: *Bu-bum bump*.

I lay flat on my back in bed. I stared at the ceiling. I wasn't sure if I was relieved that Naomi was trying to make peace (at least, that's what I *hoped* she was doing)—or even *more* upset that she had let so much time pass before deciding to finish our conversation.

In the end, though, I guess I'd have to say I was relieved. Because if she'd chased after me anytime sooner . . . it would have gotten ugly. I would have started screaming at her. Or throwing punches. I'd come pretty damn close already. Only in the past five minutes had I relaxed enough to unclench my fists.

"Dave?" she called.

"What?"

"Can I come in?"

"You're gonna come in anyway," I grumbled.

She opened the door and quietly sat at the foot of my mattress, careful to avoid touching me. "Dave . . . I . . . I had no idea."

"About *what*?"

"About the column."

"What about it?"

"I just went through some of the old e-mails on the server," she said. "I mean, I really *read* them. Not just what the kids wrote, but what *you* wrote back to them, too. And not what got printed in the school paper, either. What you answered on your own."

"Yeah?" I asked. "So?"

At the end there, she'd started slipping into her Infinitely Wiser Older Sister tone. It was *not* what I needed to hear. I didn't need to feel like a kindergartener for the millionth time this week. I kept my eyes fixed squarely on the overhead light.

"I've been . . . I just—I wanted to tell you," she said.

"Oh." I laughed. "Thanks for sharing. Is that it?"

"No. I wanted to tell you that I've been incredibly unfair."

"I agree." I propped myself up on my elbows and looked at her for the first time since she'd come in. "What else—"

I broke off. Maybe I shouldn't have been *quite* so harsh. She looked terrible. Her eyes were red and puffy. She blinked, staring down at a scrunched-up bit of blanket she was anxiously fiddling with.

"I just never realized how much I've been using you and all the kids who write in," she went on. "I just got so wrapped up in being successful after feeling so low for so many months. You know? I thought I had this big shot at stardom or something. But it's so stupid. I was being totally selfish. I just want . . . We can bag the whole thing. I don't care about starting some magazine or being a local celebrity or *any* of that. It's all BS. I was just desperate. I just needed a job. I needed to feel good about myself, you know? And Joel and Brian helped. No, no, no—*you* helped. This column helped."

"But you'll *get* a job," I murmured. "You graduated cum laude."

She laughed, sniffling. "You're sweet. But this isn't about *me*. This is about *you*. Because you did so much . . . and what I'm trying to say is, I apologize. And I'll support you in whatever you want to do. It's up to you. I'll help you any way I can."

I shook my head. "So . . . what do you mean?"

"I . . ." She gazed down at the covers bunched in her hands as if they could somehow provide the cue card, the lines she needed. "You said that you wanted to quit. And maybe now's the time. You have every right to quit. I mean, maybe people will be forgiving, you know? You really did do a good thing. You helped people."

All at once, *my* eyes were stinging. This was not good.

"I didn't help people, Naomi," I muttered. "I just made a bunch of stuff up that I thought sounded good—"

"No, you *didn't!*" she cried, looking up at me. She laughed, wiping her eyes. "I know you, Dave. This is *me,* remember! You can't BS me. You may say that, even to yourself . . . but I know you cared. You said you wanted to be honest, and it shows."

"How?" I said. The word barely squeezed out. I wasn't even talking to my sister anymore; I think I was mostly talking to myself. "By lying? By being a hypocrite?"

She shook her head vigorously. "You were *never* a hypocrite—"

"Naomi, you want to know what I did?" I interrupted. "I spent every afternoon chatting online with Celeste Fanucci. And I didn't even *know* it was Celeste Fanucci. But that's not the point. . . . See, at the end of every night, when I had to write the column, I would just pull something out of my ass—about being *honest,* about confronting *fears,* about seeking *support* . . . and all this crap, and you know what the worst thing is? A, my advice was totally lame; B, I never followed any of it myself; and C, I used the whole thing to hide from my *biggest* problem—which is that my life sucks. Because *I'm* too much of a wuss to go out and make new friends. *That's* the truth."

Naomi was silent for a few seconds.

"It wasn't lame," she finally whispered. "I read what you wrote. It *wasn't* lame."

A tear dropped from my cheek. I hadn't even realized I was crying. I *hated* crying in front of my sister. Luckily, I didn't do it very often. I hadn't done it in over a year—not since Mom had stupidly rented a movie called *Leaving Las Vegas* starring Nicolas Cage, who sort of looks like my dad did before he died, which is about a guy who drinks himself to death, and we'd *all* cried. But that's not the point, either.

"I have to quit," I breathed. "That's all there is to it. I can't go on like this."

Naomi nodded. "I know, Dave. So what do you want to do?"

"Maybe you should let me give that speech at school on Monday—the one *you're* supposed to give," I said, half jokingly. I rubbed my eyes with my fists. "I mean, why not? Brian wants to know who the real Naomi is, right? I might as well go out with a bang."

"Uh . . ." Naomi chuckled uncomfortably.

I almost chuckled, too. I could picture the horror: Brian What's-His-Face shows up with a ten-strong press junket from the *Village Voice*, camera flashes snapping—and Joel Newbury is front and center with Principal Fairfax (a man who I rarely see, but who strikes terror in me whenever I do because his old forehead is always wrinkled like a dried-up washcloth—as if he's constantly thirsty and irritable, on the verge of snapping). Not to mention the fact they're sitting right beside Celeste Fanucci, *and* Hafida Al-Saif, *and* S.O.M.B, whoever she really is . . .

One thing was for sure. If I wanted to stop hiding and follow my own advice, this was the way to do it. I'd reveal myself—in utter nakedness. As buck naked (symbolically at least) as Mrs. Slotnick across the street from Grandpa Meyer . . .

"Yeah," I found myself saying.

"Yeah what?" Naomi asked.

"I *will* do it," I announced.

Remarkably, I felt better. Simply uttering the words made me feel as if I'd just wriggled out of a straitjacket.

I had to hold on to that feeling. I had to *cling* to it.

"Don't tell anybody anything," I said. "Not even Joel. Pretend you're gonna come on Monday. But don't. Stay at home. I'll make the speech myself. I'll tell everybody who Naomi really is. I'll end it once and for all."

Naomi bit her lip. "Uh . . . are you sure?"

"I'm sure."

"And you don't want me to come at *all*? Not even for moral support?"

"Is it Joel? Is that what you're worried about?"

She nodded. "I just . . . He's gonna be really mad."

I wouldn't have believed it possible, but I actually felt for her in this situation. Then again, she'd been scarred. She'd had "chicken pox." The circumstances were beyond her control.

"Okay, okay. You can tell Joel. If you want, tell him five minutes before I go on. I'm just worried he—"

"No, no," she gently interrupted. "Really. Don't worry about anything. If this is the way you want to do it . . . I'll handle Joel. But remember, Dave. People out there count on you. And they might get mad. But if they *do* get mad, it's only because they cared so much about how you helped them. It's only because you meant so much to them. So, in a way, the madder they get, the more you'll realize—"

"Hey, Naomi?" I said.

"Yeah?"

"I think we should both quit while we're ahead. I need to take a nap. We're both probably gonna need a lot of shut-eye this weekend, you know?"

She smiled through her tears. "Maybe you're right," she said. "But who says *shut-eye*?"

TELL IT TO NAOMI—
IN PERSON!

We've all wondered. We've all speculated.
Hey, some of us have even placed bets!
(Don't worry: no names will
be mentioned here. ☺)
But now is our big chance . . .

Meet the real Naomi!

WHEN: 3:45 today
WHERE: The school auditorium
WHY: So she can introduce herself, answer
your questions, and talk about what it means
to be a famous advice columnist!

BE THERE!

NOTE: All athletic practices and
extracurricular activities will be
postponed one hour.

Chapter Twenty-two

The scene in the auditorium on Monday wasn't *quite* the way I'd pictured it, but it was frighteningly close. It was worse in some ways. It was more crowded than I'd thought it would be. I honestly didn't believe so many people would stick around after school if they didn't have to. Lord knows *I* always bolted the instant the bell rang. Almost every folding chair was occupied, mostly with girls. And faculty. (Who would have guessed Mr. Cooper would come? What did *he* care about advice columns? He was an algebra teacher.) There must have been four hundred people there. And in tribute to my nightmare fantasy, Brian What's-His-Face really *was* sitting front row center with Joel Newbury and Principal Fairfax.

At least he didn't have a ten-strong press junket. He *did* have a camera, though.

I hid on the side of the stage, poking my head through the curtains.

It was almost four o'clock. The room was humming. The audience was fidgety. Why wouldn't they be? They were all waiting for Naomi. *Especially* Joel. He kept frowning and glancing at his watch. I couldn't bring myself to step out and get started, though. My feet were firmly rooted to the floor. It's one thing to feel empowered after some kind of supposed revelation—a revelation, mind you, I'd had after I'd been up all night and learned my grandpa was a degenerate fiend and discovered that Celeste . . .

Dammit.

There she was.

I'd figured Celeste would come—of course she would—but I hadn't spotted her until now. She was sitting in the last row, near the exit, wearing that same green polka-dotted dress she'd worn the day I first spoke to her. How fitting. How symbolic. Ha, ha. Ironic, too! Because I hadn't even been looking for her. (Not entirely.) No, when I hadn't been panicking or staring at the clock, I'd been searching the crowd for Hafida. And *she* was conspicuously absent. I hadn't seen her at school today, either. So on top of all my other worries, I was nervous she might already have left Roosevelt for good.

"Psst!"

I nearly fainted.

It was Naomi. She was standing right behind me.

"What are *you* doing here?" I whispered. "You weren't supposed to—"

"Shhh," she whispered back. "Joel doesn't know anything about this."

She burst through the curtains and waved at him.

It took Joel a second to spot her—but the moment he did, he broke into a relieved smile and settled back into his chair. He elbowed Brian.

Brian raised the camera to his face.

My pulse tripled.

"That's your cue," Naomi said.

"What . . . ?"

"You think I would let you do this alone? You think I wouldn't be here for you? I'm your older sister, Dave. By seven years. When it comes to you, I do whatever I want, *whenever* I want—and *you* don't have a say in it."

I stared at her.

"Get the hell out there!" she commanded.

I nodded, swallowing.

I pushed through the curtains.

I don't know what I was thinking. It's difficult to describe. Those twelve or so steps to the front of the stage constitute—by *far*—one of the most surreal moments of my life. All I remember was a dead silence: the kind of silence you only experience in the boondocks. In New York there's always *something:* a voice, a radio, a car horn . . . but as I walked up to the lectern the entire city seemed to shut down and hold its breath.

"Hi," I said.

Joel Newbury stood. He glared at Naomi.

I didn't see how Naomi responded—but whatever she did, Joel sat down.

I took a deep breath and looked over the crowd.

"I know you're all waiting for Naomi," I announced. Shockingly, my voice was fairly steady. "And it's funny. I mean seeing as it's Halloween and all . . . it's normally a time when we put *on* costumes. But today I'm flipping it. I'm taking off my costume. What I'm trying to say is that if you want Naomi, you've got her. *I'm* Naomi."

I waited.

The announcement didn't seem to be sinking in.

I could feel four hundred pairs of eyes on me, but nobody reacted. Nobody even *peeped.* This was more than boondocks silence. This was cemetery silence. Maybe I needed to stop trying to be clever. I was never very good at it, anyway.

"Well, let me tell you a story," I said. "See, when you guys first started writing in to the column, I . . . well, I thought of it like a reality TV show. I figured the only reason you liked it was because you liked to gawk, to revel in each other's misfortune. To rag on each other. I figured all the kids at this school are jerks, right? They're so psyched when somebody else is embarrassed. They're so psyched when somebody else is suffering. But it didn't take me long to realize that I was totally wrong. *Totally wrong.* It wasn't that at all. It was the *opposite.* You people . . . you people are honest and open—and you root for each other. You were fans of the column because you're *fans of each other.* And . . . um, so—I just wanted to say . . . I'm gonna miss writing it. I'm gonna miss my regulars. Because as of today, it's closed for business. But that doesn't mean you are. Because you all are the real deal. So I'm sorry. I'm really, really, really sorry."

Now the auditorium wasn't as quiet anymore.

A murmur rippled through the crowd.

It grew louder and louder.

My heart began to thump again.

Now they got it.

I glanced at the back row.

Celeste stood up. She stared right at me. The look on her face was about as close to pure revulsion as I'd ever seen. She stormed out.

"Wait!" I yelled at her. "Hold on—"

I felt a hand clamp around my arm.

It belonged to Joel Newbury.

"I don't know what you and your sister are trying to pull here, but you're both in big trouble," he said through clenched teeth.

Principal Fairfax appeared onstage beside him.

"My office, fifteen minutes," he snapped at me.

"Uh . . . okay."

Suddenly the stage was crawling with people. I couldn't get a grip on the situation. Time seemed to accelerate. Naomi ran out and started pleading with both Joel and the principal—but about what, I don't know. I didn't even hear what she was saying. All I know is that somewhere in the fracas, Joel let go of me.

I took the opportunity to dash backstage.

So, I'll probably be expelled, I thought, crouching low in the shadows. *Maybe even thrown in some kind of juvenile prison. But, hey, I bet I can make myself useful there! People in prison need advice, don't they? Sure—*

Naomi poked her head through the curtains. She smiled at me.

"Dave, I'll meet you at home, okay?" she whispered quickly. "I'll soften Mom and Aunt Ruth up. So don't you worry. I'm so proud of you. I love—"

"Naomi!" somebody barked, grabbing her. "This isn't the story I wanted. . . ."

Her face vanished.

The curtains fluttered shut.

Okay, I told myself. *Okay. Just relax.*

I knew I had to look on the bright side, being the eternal optimist that I was. At least Naomi hadn't completed her last sentence in front of four hundred people.

***

I was less than twenty feet from Principal Fairfax's office when I heard footsteps behind me in the hall.

I picked up my pace.

The footsteps grew louder.

Crap. There was no use trying to escape. I knew what was coming, too: one of those girls out in the auditorium had waited for me as I'd hid backstage for twenty minutes, and then had followed me as I'd snuck through the halls—no, *wormed* my way through the halls (*to worm* being the only verb fitting for a worm)—and now she was about to bawl me out or slap me around.

And I deserved it.

I should consider myself lucky, though. If I only had to deal with one furious tirade or act of violence before I was expelled, I'd be getting off *easy.* Everybody in that auditorium wanted to bawl me out or slap me around. But even so, I'd be lying if I said I didn't feel like a criminal awaiting the guillotine. I hung my head. I steeled myself and turned . . .

And found myself face to face with Olga Romanoff.

"What's up, Naomi?" she said flatly.

I swallowed. "Hey."

"That was a nice scam you pulled," she said.

"I know. I'm sorry. Really."

"Yeah, that's what you said back in the auditorium." Surprisingly, she sounded bemused. "Some speech you gave."

"Uh . . ."

"You know what the weird thing is?" she asked. "I finally got rid of him. Your advice helped. I can't believe it, but it did. I mean, damn. Who would have ever thought that a little punk like you could help somebody like me? Look at you! How could *you* help *me*?"

Help?

I blinked, not comprehending in the least. "I don't know," I squeaked. "That's good, though . . . I guess? That I helped you? Right?"

"Right," she said. "I guess."

"Uh . . . which 'him' is this, if you don't mind my asking? I'm sorry—"

"My boyfriend." Her dark eyes bored directly into my own.

I wracked my brains trying to figure out who or what she was talking about. But all I could manage to say—in classic idiotic Dave Rosen fashion—was "*You* have a boyfriend?"

"Yes, it *is* hard to believe, isn't it?" she asked sarcastically.

"No, no." My face turned bright red. "God, I'm sorry, I didn't mean it like that at all. It's just—I—I mean, I've never seen you with a . . . uh—well, I just always see you with those chicks from the lit—sorry, girls from the lit club."

She laughed. "You know something? You're a lot more articulate in e-mails than you are in person. You talk like a dope."

"I . . ." On second thought, a guillotine might have been preferable to this. "I guess I do," I mumbled.

"My boyfriend—my *ex*-boyfriend—goes to Franklin," she said. "That's why you never saw him. But you *do* know him."

"I do?"

"You know him through me. I'll give you a hint. He smells. He told me not to buy candy for the Halloween party, because he thought it would make me fatter than I already am. He wanted to sneak beer into the party instead. I was very . . . 'sick of' him." She made air quotes.

Holy—

She might as well *have* slapped me.

"*You?*" I shrieked, my eyes bulging. "*You're* S.O.M.B?"

She laughed again. "I guess now the artist formerly known as," she replied.

"Bu-but—But you're not *fat!*" I sputtered, looking her up and down. (Okay, I admit to having compared her to one of those wooden Russian dolls, but they aren't so much fat as stout. Or *solid.*) "You don't have a beard of zits! I hardly see any zits at all! Three, on your chin! Tiny ones!"

"Gee, you really know how to sweet-talk a lady," she said as dryly as ever.

"I . . . no . . . ugh." If I blushed any more, my face would explode. "All right. Forget that you *aren't* fat and ugly—because you really aren't. You act totally different in e-mails than you do in person. I mean, come on. You can't blame me for being surprised, can you?"

Her eyes narrowed, but she was grinning. "Hello? Isn't this a case of the pot calling the kettle black?" She gave me a quick once-over. "I'm looking at you, and I'm not seeing a woman named Naomi. I'd say you acted a little differently in e-mails too, there, buddy. Who should be surprised here?"

I shook my head hopelessly. "But you never mentioned books or anything when you wrote in! You never mentioned the lit club, either! You never mentioned that coffee shop—"

"And you never mentioned being a guy," she shot back.

"Yeah, but . . ." Air flowed from my lungs. I wasn't even sure why I was arguing. I didn't know what I was *thinking.* I was too deflated.

"Listen, I don't mean to give you a hard time," she said. "Well, maybe a little." She patted my shoulder, teasingly. "Okay. I know you feel like an asshole—actually, I don't know *how* you feel. Hey, have you ever read that book by the guy who pretended to be . . . ? Oh, never mind. I just want to say this: don't worry about me. I'm cool. A little freaked out, yes—but cool. But you shouldn't be surprised about *me,* either. I mean, just because I'm in the lit club doesn't mean . . . Forget it. Just go back and read what we wrote to each other. I bet things will start to make sense. You'll see."

I nodded, staring down at the floor. Once again, I didn't have the

slightest idea what she was talking about. I only knew that I really *must* have been deflated—or at least overwhelmed—because there was a good chance I might start crying. And that had been happening *way* too much lately.

"Did you keep the e-mails I sent you?" she asked quietly.

I looked up. "Yeah, of course. They were some of my favorites...." I swallowed.

"Well, good. Because I kept the ones you sent—"

Principal Fairfax's door crashed open.

Oh, God.

He hadn't just been waiting for me. He'd been *stewing*. Compared to how his forehead had looked back in the auditorium . . . this was beyond cracked-up washcloth material. Now it looked like a giant raisin: a bright red one.

"Go in and sit down." He stepped aside and shot a sour glance at Olga. "And you, young lady—go home."

Olga's eyes met mine.

"Good luck," she mouthed.

"Thanks," I whispered in return.

A smile spread across my face.

"Now!" Principal Fairfax spat.

He grabbed my shirt and yanked me into the office.

I managed to catch one last glimpse of Olga. She smiled back at me, puzzled. She was probably wondering how I could possibly manage to look so cheerful, given the circumstances.

It wasn't because she'd wished me luck.

It was because for a moment there, she'd made the possibility of expulsion seem like a crisis that maybe—just maybe—I could cope with. Or try to cope with, anyway.

She'd helped.

And really, who would have ever thought that somebody like Olga Romanoff could help a little punk like me?

Chapter Twenty-three ▬▬▬

The verdict: four days' suspension.

The upshot: massive relief.

I'll spare you the details of what went on inside Principal Fairfax's office. (Enraged rants are never very interesting.) Suffice it to say that he basically recapped everything I'd been telling myself for the past month—that I was a liar, that I had some serious apologizing to do to every single person who'd written to me, that I'd betrayed the school's trust, et cetera. He concluded by telling me that "*honesty* and *honor code* come from the same root" and that I should think about that during my absence.

I told him I would.

And I meant it.

I *wanted* to think about honesty.

Unfortunately, by the time I reached 433 East Ninth Street, I had other worries on my mind—namely my mother and my aunt.

Suspension beat expulsion, no doubt about it. Punishment-wise, they weren't even in the same ballpark. But I couldn't really see myself putting such a positive spin on the day's events for Mom and Aunt Ruth. ("Just think, you guys! I'll have the rest of the week off to help you do chores around the house!") And I knew that whatever fury Principal Fairfax had unleashed on me back at school . . . well, *that* was just an appetizer before the main course. What waited for me upstairs was a Don Vito's–sized serving of pure, unadulterated wrath.

The front door of the apartment building suddenly flew open. "Dude!"

Cheese barreled down the steps, shaking his head. It was clear he'd been waiting in the lobby for me. Before I could manage a word, he grabbed my arm and hustled me down the street.

"I wouldn't go up there if I were you," he warned. He laughed shakily. "I . . . uh . . . I'd let your mom and aunt settle down a little bit."

"Oh," I said. I decided not to question why he was making the effort to tell me this, considering we were barely friends anymore. In times of emergency, it's usually best just to run with the situation.

"I could hear them all the way down in my apartment," he said.

I swallowed. "What are they doing?"

Cheese paused at the end of the block, glancing over his shoulder. "They aren't listening to Hendrix, I'll tell you that," he muttered.

"Did . . . um . . ."

"They're freaking out on Naomi," he said.

Uh-oh. I gazed back at the building, rubbing my moist palms on my jeans. "Did you hear what they were saying?"

"Something about 'the column, the column.' That was all I really understood."

"Oh." I looked down.

"I know about the column, Dave," he said.

My head jerked up. "What?"

"I know that you're Naomi, too."

Blood pounded toward my skull. "Uh . . . did you just, uh—?"

"Did you really think *you* could fool *me?*" he interrupted. He laughed indignantly, folding his jacketed arms across his chest. "I thought you'd give me a little more credit than that, Dave. We go back a long ways."

"But . . . But . . ." I couldn't speak.

"Come on," he said. "The Bad Kid had the exact same problems as *I* did, but only in chick form. You know what I'm saying?"

I gaped at him.

The blood in my head abruptly made a U-turn. My face went white. Finding out that Olga Romanoff was S.O.M.B. was one thing.

That I could believe. (Sort of. I was still grappling with it.) But this . . . No. *This* was as if a cache of homemade tattoo ink *had* exploded at the Spiral Lounge. This was a case of strange forces conspiring against me *twice* in a row. Back to back. This was too much.

"You?" I croaked. "You're the . . ."

Cheese laughed again. "Come on! You *know* me. I have a taste for the unexpected. I get freaky in all sorts of ways—ways the average man can't fathom. But I did feel a little funny about pretending to be a chick. That is, until I realized that *you* were doing it, too. Then I was like, hey! Maybe *every* sick visionary has to pretend to be a chick in order to reach that Higher Level of Being. I mean, I always maintained that you don't talk like other guys. But in this case, you went *deep,* son. Deep. You made me go deep, too. You know what I'm saying?"

I started laughing. I couldn't help myself.

"No, Cheese," I said. "I don't know what you're saying."

"Let me put it this way: yes, I have a crush on your sister. I admit it. Can you blame me? She's hot! She's a sexy, high-style *woman,* son! But it's not like I'm *pining* over her or anything. She's practically *my* sister, too!"

I shook my head. "Cheese, I'm—"

"Whoa, whoa, whoa, let me finish. I'm on a roll. See, I overheard Naomi talking with her boyfriend out on the stoop one day. You know, about the column. Oh—by the way, her boyfriend is chump change, right? And I'm a bank-issued stack of crisp hundreds? But anyway, I thought, damn, she stole my idea! I want my fifteen percent! No, but seriously, I was like, I should do something here. I should write in and ask *her* for advice. Because I *need* advice. I need to know why the hell things got so screwed up between you and me. And who better to answer *that* but your sister? So that's what I did. But I couldn't write in as a *guy,* because guys don't write in to advice columns. But as soon as you wrote back . . . I knew. *That's* why I acted so weird when I saw you on Friday and Saturday. *I* knew, but I didn't know if *you* knew. You know?"

I nodded.

I wasn't sure what else to do.

That stupid lump started to creep up my throat again. If it hadn't belonged there before, it *definitely* didn't belong there now. I tried to gulp it back down. My brain was like a slot machine, whirring with a blur of dialogue I'd been craving to start for the past month. How long had he felt bad about all this? Did this mean we were really friends again, the same way we were before? And along those lines, did he want to introduce me to his *new* friends?

But of all the burning questions, the loser that came up was:

"How come you didn't invite me to the party?"

I couldn't believe it. Forget getting rid of the lump: I needed that Cosmic Rewind Button.

Cheese sighed. "I . . . I don't know."

Neither of us spoke.

After a minute he looked at me.

"I've said it before, and I'll say it again, Dave. 'The mind is a terrible thing. The mind is a *terrible* thing.'"

"You're telling me," I mumbled. I drew in a shaky breath. "Sorry about that. But listen, um—here's something I want to say. This band you're starting . . . if you want a built-in mailing list, I've got the e-mail addresses of about four hundred chicks."

His eyes lit up. "Dude! That is *huge*—"

"I'm kidding, Cheese. But I am psyched to check you guys out. I think my next big gig will be as a rock critic. You know . . . a rock critic with a mission—one who hates singer/songwriters but who loves real bands, especially bands with live onstage gravy incidents. I'm through as an advice columnist. And I definitely need a second job. Going to school by itself just doesn't cut it anymore."

He smiled. It was the same kind of smile I'd given Olga Romanoff. "Dave! You're a freaking genius! You just came up with our band name!"

"I did?"

"Yeah! The Gravy Incident! Oh, man, I knew you had skills, but this takes the cake. . . . So now you *have* to review us. And you'll have to meet all the band members in person, right? It's the only way you can get the full, decadent, debauched history of the Gravy Incident's formation."

"Well, yeah, of course," I said. "I definitely have to meet them all. I'm especially interested in how your guitarist doesn't have a guitar that works . . . but I guess I'll just have to let him use mine. I have a real guitar: the same kind of guitar that Hendrix played at Woodstock. See, that's how I intend to scandalize you—by giving you your band name *and* lending you my guitar, and then putting it all in print."

Cheese brushed his bangs out of his face. "That is a *sick* story, son!" he cried excitedly. "Mike can smash his *own* lame guitar at our first gig. At my birthday party! And then he'll have to play yours. Then, when you see the Gravy Incident play . . . well, we're *both* gonna go far. You'll take us to the top. It'll be like when *Rolling Stone* gave the White Stripes five stars. It'll be a seminal event in rock history."

"Right," I said. My voice was strained. No matter how hard I tried to swallow, that lump wouldn't recede. It had a mind of its own. I just had to ignore it. "I, just . . . uh, I'm worried I won't be allowed to come to the party. I don't see Mom and Aunt Ruth letting me have fun anytime in the foreseeable future."

"But they can chaperone you," Cheese protested. "They'll probably want to chaperone you, anyway, right? They already think I'm the Bad Kid."

I finally managed to smile back at him. "Is that how you came up with that alias?"

Cheese shrugged. "I don't know. The Bad Dude, the Bad Son, the Bad Kid—it's all real. You know what I'm saying?"

"No, Cheese. I don't. You sound like an idiot."

He stared at me.

Then he laughed.

I laughed, too. And I *kept* laughing. I couldn't stop. Neither could he. We stood there on the street corner, cracking up like two jackasses. I really hoped Mom and Aunt Ruth wouldn't come looking for me. This was not something they needed to see.

In true Cheese form, though, his freakish dialect had also inadvertently reminded me of something serious and profound—something that required my immediate attention. There was somebody *else* I needed to talk to, somebody else who was as "real" (and incomprehensible) as he was. And I needed to talk to her *now,* while I still had a chance, before I was grounded for the rest of my natural life and perhaps beyond.

"Look, I got an errand to run," I said. "A couple, actually. By way of Mott Street and a bookstore."

"Right on," Cheese said.

He hesitated. Then he extended a hand, overhand style.

I shook it.

He pulled me in for a hug.

"Hey, if *you* can't make it to my party, at least make sure Naomi comes," he joked quietly, clapping me on the back. "It'll be good for the Gravy Incident's image if we have hot chicks at our parties. You know? Real hot chicks, I mean. Not just weird dudes who pretend to be chicks for the sake of secretly writing each other notes."

"I hear you, son," I replied. "I'll see what I can do. I'll see what I can do."

***

This time, there was no hassle at St. Vincent's: no questions, no accusing glares. I knew the routine. I handed over my ID to the security guard—another grandmotherly woman—and told her I was visiting Mr. Al-Saif, a patient on the sixth floor.

She slid the book across the desk.

I signed my name and headed to the elevator.

I was legit.

I had a plan this time, too. I had *gifts*—by way of introduction. Not to pat myself on the back or anything, but this was a pretty classy move. *Dignitaries* gave gifts. *Ambassadors. Diplomats.* Which made sense, seeing as Hospital Girl and I were from different countries.

Clutched tightly in both my hands was a plastic bag filled with the spoils of the errands I'd run over the past hour: a spanking-new copy of *The Sneetches and Other Stories,* by Dr. Seuss, and two compilation cassette tapes I'd found in a two-dollar bin on Mott Street,

The Best of Yo! MTV Raps and an old *Jimi Hendrix Greatest Hits* collection.

I would celebrate our common bonds, and I would pay tribute to her taste.

And then I would turn her on to mine.

I would make *friends*. I would make *peace*. (I admit: mostly with myself.) It wasn't just classy; it was smooth.

The elevator doors opened. I stepped out onto the sixth floor—Hospital Girl's couch was deserted.

Huh. I don't know why I'd assumed she would be curled up there again, listening to her Walkman. I hurried to the nurses' station. That same sour old security guard was working the desk—the one who'd watched me as I'd bolted the last time.

"Hi," I said to him as politely as possible. "Can you tell me which room Mr. Al-Saif is staying in, please?"

He glanced down at a clipboard.

"Al-Saif checked out yesterday," he said.

"Excuse me?"

"He checked out."

"I . . . uh . . . *Why?*"

"I don't know," the guard said.

My grip tightened on the plastic bag. "I . . . Uh, do you know where he went?"

He shook his head. "No. And even if I did, I couldn't tell you. It just says here that he's ended his stay."

I felt a sinking sensation in my gut. "That's it?"

"Well, no." He laughed gruffly and glanced up. "His daughter is coming by sometime to settle the bill. But I'm not holding my breath. She told me she was leaving New York in the next few days—she said something about going to live with her mother in France. At least, that's what I think she told me. She was a chatty one, but I never understood half of what she was saying."

My hopes rose. "Did she say when she was coming back here?"

"No. Your guess is as good as mine."

"I . . ."

I turned to the clock above the elevator. It was already 5:15. Not good. I'd been suspended. I was supposed to be *home*. Mom and Aunt Ruth had probably already notified the police that I was missing. Either that or they'd given up and put a contract out on my life with a professional killer.

"You can leave a note for her," the guard offered. "I'll make sure she gets it if she ever shows up."

"Really?" I turned back around. A note seemed sort of impersonal, but at this point, I didn't have a choice. I had to do *something*. I thought of the words I'd written to Hospital Girl: *There are no simple solutions.* I'd never imagined those words would come back to bite me in the butt, but here I was.

Still, on one level, I'd been right . . . hadn't I? Or was I just rationalizing, making an excuse for not being able to talk to her in person? Maybe it was a combination of both. Maybe that sort of feeble advice, as in "You always have to make the best of a crummy situation"—especially when you give it to yourself—is the only way you can *deal* with a crummy situation. Sometimes it's the only way you can survive. It's the only way you can keep from going bonkers.

"You know, thanks—I think I will leave a note," I said.

The security guard tore a blank page from his clipboard and shoved it across the desk, along with a chewed-up ballpoint.

Dear Hospital Girl,

I came here to say hi in person, and I guess to say goodbye, too, but it didn't quite work out. Sorry about that. From what I hear, though, it sounds like you're going back home to be with your mom, and that's a good thing.

I'm used to writing on the keyboard, where I can erase everything and go back and make myself sound smart and witty, but here I just have to write whatever comes to my mind and make sure it counts. I'm pressed for time. I could have learned something from you because everything _you_ wrote counted. You kept it real because you were nobody but yourself, as you said. And that is cool, Hospital Girl. It is cooler than I can tell you, and I can't think of another word besides cool because I am lame and distracted and corny and about to be in serious trouble. The slang for it, I believe, is "royally screwed."

So I won't try to write any more. Here are some things I wanted to give you as parting gifts. I think they are all self-explanatory (that is a big term, you might need to look it up ☺) except the Hendrix tape. I love Hendrix. That is why I am giving it to you. I want to share something of me with you. I told you I was corny. I fear that makes not sense?

Ha, ha.

You won't be able to write to me anymore at the old e-mail address, but you can write to me at drosen@webmail.com. PLEASE write. Tell me what you think of Dr. Seuss and Hendrix. Tell me about Papa, too.

We can talk about that stuff now.

And good luck.

Naomi

P.S. My real name is Dave.

I hesitated for a moment, debating whether to read it over, and then glanced back at the clock. It was 5:25. Mom and Aunt Ruth had definitely hired a hit squad by now. *Screw it.* When had I ever second-guessed myself? I folded the paper and handed to the guard—and tossed him the plastic shopping bag, too.

"Thanks again," I said. "You'll make sure she gets all this?"

He shrugged. "If she ever shows," he said.

"She'll show. She's honest."

"Oh, she is, huh? What makes you so sure?"

"I know her," I said.

He sniffed. "All right."

"Please make sure—"

"She'll *get* it," he interrupted. "You said she's honest, right?"

"Yeah. Thanks."

I turned and dashed back to the elevator.

As I waited for the doors to open, I thought about how funny it was that I'd used the word *honest*. Not "ha-ha" funny, but funny in the sense that it reminded me for certain that I was a dead man. Because I still had one more crucial errand to run if *I* was to be honest (true to Principal Fairfax's request)—which meant I wouldn't get home until eight o'clock or so . . . which, in turn, meant that Mom and Aunt Ruth wouldn't just kill me; they'd embark on a cross-country tour with my carcass as a warning to all kids who had the gall to come home past dinnertime after they'd just been suspended for four days.

But it was best not to overanalyze these sorts of things.

Besides, I didn't have any rational guidance to offer myself. My career as an advice columnist was over.

Chapter Twenty-four

"Yes? Who is it?"

I shoved my face into the buzzer speaker. "It's Dave Rosen. A friend of Celeste's from school."

There was a pause.

Even through a crappy intercom—and after only four words—I could tell that Celeste's father *was* a conservative research scientist. I almost smiled in appreciation, except for the fact that I was out of my mind.

"One moment," Dr. Fanucci replied.

Celeste lived in a brownstone on Eighteenth Street. It hadn't been hard to find her. I knew she lived near Union Square, and there were only four Fanuccis in Manhattan. All it took was one 411 call. And now—

The buzzer crackled with static.

"Yeah?"

It was her voice.

"It's Dave, Celeste!" I yelled.

"I know," she replied.

The words were garbled. They sounded more like *"Eye Oh—KKCCH."*

"Hey . . . um, can you come down here?" I yelled. I smiled, even though she couldn't see me. "I feel like we're on the train to DeKalb Avenue."

There was no answer.

I squeezed my eyes shut.

Why did I have to bring up DeKalb Avenue? That was beyond corny. It was beyond cheesy. It was the *lamest* possible attempt to reestablish our nonexistent relationship—

The lock clicked.

Celeste opened the front door. She wasn't wearing her green polka-dotted dress anymore. She'd changed into sweats. Her blond curls were stuffed under a wool cap.

"Hi," I said.

"Zeke dumped me," she said.

"Oh." If this was a test, I'd failed. I knew she wanted me to react in a certain way, but I was too dense. "I . . ."

"He was cheating on me the whole time. It was with some chick he met at the Spiral Lounge the very first time he played there."

I laughed.

"I'm glad you find this funny," she said.

"No. I'm sorry. It's just . . . the way you said *chick*. It reminded me—"

"It was a word I got from Naomi," Celeste interrupted.

I looked at her.

She shook her head. Her lips quivered.

"Celeste, I—"

"Naomi was my best friend, you know that?" she said in a strained voice. "Naomi was my *best friend*. And I'm gonna miss her so much, because now I don't *have* a best friend. I don't have a boyfriend, either. I don't have a damn thing."

I stared down at my sneakers.

"You know what's funny, Dave?" she whispered. "I used to think that when you *say* something—I mean, when you really spell it out—it stops being true. The truest things are always the things that are *never* said. They're the things that *can't* be said. Because when you *say* them . . . it's like, you put a piece of yourself into them. You take them out of a pure realm—a realm that exists

197

outside yourself, that exists outside of *everyone*. And that's how the real truth starts getting chipped away. See, I never *told* Naomi she was my best friend. I just knew she was. And when I finally decided to tell her . . . well, we all know what happened, right? I found out she never existed at all."

"But she did exist," I said, my voice thick. "She *does.*"

Celeste laughed sadly. "She does? Where?"

I looked up again. "Do you know why I decided to start writing an advice column?" I asked.

"I don't have the slightest idea," she said.

"It was because of you. It was because I had a crush on *you*. I knew I would never able to be talk to you, because you're . . . well, you're *you*—and so I had to figure out a way to get to you. And then when I did, when I talked to you—I mean, I stopped having a crush on you. I started having a crush on FONY. I felt like: this is *the* girl. And when you said that you were a freshman, I—"

"I never said I was a freshman," Celeste countered.

"You made it *seem* like you were," I said.

"How?"

"You know, I don't even remember. The point is . . . all right. I know *I* lied. But you weren't totally honest, either. Because the Celeste Fanucci who went out with Zeke Beck is *not* the Celeste Fanucci who wrote to Naomi."

Celeste rubbed her eyes. "How many other girls did you have crushes on, Dave?" she asked sadly.

"What?"

"Oh, come on!" she said. "It's like you wrote in your column. Crushes are fleeting. Dave . . . I know what guys think. I also know I'm lucky to look the way I look. I *know* I'm so much better off than so many girls because I don't have to worry about so much stuff that other girls worry about. *I* was an advice columnist, too, remember?"

"So why don't you act like one?" I cried.

She dropped her hands. "Excuse me?"

"You act like a ditz, Celeste! When I found out you were FONY, I couldn't believe it. Up until then, I seriously wondered if you'd gotten somebody to ghostwrite *your* columns."

She laughed. "You don't know me, Dave."

"Yeah, I do. And *you* know *me*."

"I . . . I don't even know why I'm talking to you. Forget it." She turned and opened the door. "I gotta go upstairs."

"Is that it?" I asked.

She nodded.

I shook my head. "You're wrong. I know why you're talking to me. It's because you miss Naomi. But you don't have to. She didn't go anywhere. Naomi is *me*. You still have that friendship. And no matter what, that friendship is real. No matter how much you dissect it, or talk about it, or analyze it, it'll *always* be real."

Celeste glanced over her shoulder. "So what are you saying? That we should pretend nothing happened? Grab some falafel and just start over?"

"Not start over," I said. "We should just take a different route." I hesitated, realizing that the streetlamps had just flickered on. I took a deep breath. Mom and Aunt Ruth were waiting. Four days of suspension were waiting.

"What?" Celeste asked.

"Nothing. I was just thinking we'll probably have to wait a little to start over, seeing as I probably won't be allowed out of my house for the next forty years. . . ."

For the first time all night, she smiled. "Well, we can always e-mail each other. Right?"

I smiled back. "Right," I said.

"Goodnight, Dave."

"Goodnight, Celeste."

"I . . ."

"Yes?"

"Nothing." She sighed. "I'll drop you a line tomorrow. I have something to ask my friend."

"Your friend will be waiting," I said.

Celeste nodded. "I'm glad."

She closed the door.

"I'm glad, too," I told the empty stoop.